ROMANCING THE Nerd

leah rae miller

Entangled Publishing, LLC
2614 South Timberline Road
Suite 109
Fort Collins, CO 80525

Entangled Teen is an imprint of Entangled Publishing, LLC.
Visit our website at www.entangledpublishing.com.

Edited by Stacy Abrams and Heather Howland
Cover design by LJ Anderson
Interior design by Toni Kerr

Print ISBN: 978-1633752252
Ebook ISBN: 978-1633752269

Manufactured in the United States of America

First Edition April 2016

10 9 8 7 6 5 4 3 2 1

For my husband and best friend, Shane.

Chapter One
DAN

I used to despise popular people. At the time, I had all these reasons why I hated them. My reasons were logical and seemed to apply in pretty much every situation. Let me break it down. See, high school can very often feel like going to prison. Not that I've ever been in the slammer, but if every prison movie ever made is to be trusted, then the similarities are obvious. For example, they say that on your first day of being in the pokey, one should find the biggest, meanest guy and kick his ass in order to establish dominance. In high school, one should find the goofiest, most self-conscious kid and embarrass him to the point of mental scarring.

On day one of tenth grade, Cory Granger tripped me in homeroom, causing me to face-plant spectacularly in front of everyone with last names G through K in my class. Whether he realized it or not (I'm betting on not), it was a very strategic move. These were the people I'd be seeing every morning, every day until graduation. It was like he did three years of bullying in one moment. Way to work smarter, not harder, Cory.

They also advise that jailbirds find a group of like-minded criminals so they have someone watching their backs. The same can be said about high school. During week seven of tenth grade, Trent Simmons shoved me so hard into my locker I had a padlock-shaped bruise on my upper arm for days. But my locker neighbor and fellow underappreciated student, Andy, had my back. Sort of. "Leave him alone," Andy had told Trent, redirecting Trent's ire onto himself. We had matching bruises after that.

And like prison, popular people get special treatment by the guards—a.k.a. the faculty. Like how Karen Clark, head cheerleader, just got a "Be nice" from the principal for—with no provocation— calling me a lumpy, pathetic waste of flesh. But I got two weeks of detention for responding with a colorful description of her mother's sexual exploits.

In summation, high school can suck and popular people are assholes. They get away with things a normal student doesn't. They have inflated egos and think they rule the school.

I know. I'm coming off as a little harsh, but I can say these things now because, according to those logical reasons, I should hate myself. It's confusing and it sucks and somebody kill me now, please and thank you. It wasn't like I went out on a mission to become popular. Far from it. The first time I noticed a change was when I started to slim down due to the father/son karate lessons my dad forced me into. Cindy "popular since birth" LeDeaux actually said, I kid you not, she said, "Looking good, Dan," as we passed each other in the hall at school. I nearly choked on my no-time-to-cook-this-morning-Mom breakfast, a Pop-tart peanut butter sandwich. It was all downhill from there.

The next thing I know, Dad wants nothing in the world more than for his son to play a sport. Even though I'd been known to say, "The only sports I play involve a game controller," I love my dad and couldn't let the man down. Hence I am now at basketball practice with cheerleaders ogling me. I'll admit, their giggles and coy pointing do make me stand straighter almost on instinct, but the shame of even caring a little bit what they think is like a batarang to the head. POW!

I've learned to handle it, though. It took a good year or two, but I…I don't know. Maybe I kind of like it now. Maybe not. Again, I'm a confused, self-loathing little man. Sad times.

I take a shot from the three-point line and it completely bricks, which brings me back to the here and now. My three-point average is something I'm very proud of. My coach and teammates think I should do more work in the zone (under the basket, to be clear) because of my height (stupid mid-junior-year growth spurt), but I feel like the three-pointer takes more skill and practice. And despite my newfound popularity, I still look at life as a very elaborate role-playing game. There are powers and skills to be honed before you enter the end-of-the-level boss fight. Plus, I'm still trying to get used to using these big, goofy feet. When that growth spurt hit, it was like I got a ncw body, one that was trying to play tricks on me. The simple act of getting out of my desk has become tough because of these stupid long legs. It's embarrassing.

I shoot again. Nothing but net. Level up, bitches.

"All right, guys, wrap it up and hit the showers.

Marching band's coming in," Coach Greg yells from the other end of the court. This is my favorite part of practice. Not because it's over but because our captain, who I like to call Douchebag Donovan, has the responsibility of catching the balls we throw to him and putting them on the racks. And I've taken on the personal responsibility of throwing the basketballs at him as hard as possible. Don't worry, the guy deserves it. Besides his always-popped collar and how he says "sitch" instead of "situation," there's the fact that I've never heard him utter a kind word. Even when he's describing which girls he likes, he's a sexist d-bag. I'm no expert on the fairer sex, but I can't see any girl taking being called "doable" as a compliment.

The marching band files into the gym lugging instruments and backpacks and those big hats with the feathers on top and harnesses for said instruments. I feel for them, I really do. The tuba player, a girl named Zelda Potts who used to be a good friend of mine, is bringing up the rear and having a hell of a time trying to manage all her junk and push open the big metal door at the same time. The thing about Zelda is she's very easy to spot in a crowd. She's the quintessential ginger with her bright red hair and freckle-speckled pale skin.

And if you can't find her because of her red hair, all you have to do is look for the strangest yet most interesting outfit and she'll be wearing it. We've known each other since grade school, and she's kind of my ideal girl. She's smart, quick-witted, and her eyes are so big and doe-like I could just take a swim in them. But don't tell her I said all that because she hates my guts.

If you can't find her by her outlandish fashion sense, then look for her tuba. Why she ever decided to take up that cumbersome instrument is a mystery, considering her short stature.

The other thing about Zelda is she's so easy to get riled up. Always has been, and it's been even easier since she took offense to that one time I had to bail on her, hence the hating of my guts. Usually the best part of my day is seeing her reaction when I say something I know will get her dander up. Her eyes flash with fury and it's a mighty thing to behold.

I decide to toss Donovan one last basketball missile then go help/annoy Zelda, even though I know she'll probably tell me to GTFO. But then a thing happens. A very bad thing.

I've always had strong opinions on new shoes. I hate them with a passion. They never fit as well as your last pair and they never fail to cause blisters during the breaking-in process. Plus, they're literally walking sources of anxiety because, from the moment you first put them on, you're constantly worried about getting them dirty. And now I have a whole new reason to hate them. Since I know this will be my last chance to really make Donovan's hands sting until the next practice, I put my whole body into this final throw. But I'm wearing new shoes. Their grip on the polished court is ridiculous, and I trip slightly when I chuck the ball. The thing goes way off target.

"Zelda, look out!" someone yells from the bleachers.

She turns just in time to put her nose in the basketball's direct line of fire. It hits so hard her feather hat flies from her head and clatters across the floor along with all the other stuff she was carrying. Her hands go to her face as she doubles over in pain. A chorus of horrified gasps from the band and a few of the players is followed by loud guffaws from some of the Douchebag's lackeys.

I get to her at the same time as her friend Beth. We both put a worried hand on her back and ask in unison, "Are you okay?" which I've always thought is the stupidest question to ask someone who's just been hurt, and yet it's reflex.

A drop of blood hits the gym floor, and I've never felt so shitty in my entire life. Zelda and I have some things between us, sure, but those things have never included bodily harm.

"Dan, what the hell did you do that for? What's wrong with you, man?" Donovan asks as he passes us and goes into the locker room. Of course he knows I didn't do it on purpose. He just wants to stir the pot with his big douchey spoon.

My mouth drops open as I turn to Beth. She scowls at me. And by "scowls," I mean she gives me such a fierce look of hatred I'm pretty sure she just took ten years off my life.

I can't form a complete sentence. "But…I didn't mean… He's…"

Zelda shoves her forearm into my stomach and I stumble back. I wish she'd hit me or something. Maybe then I wouldn't feel like the lowest creature to ever crawl the planet because we'd be even… No, I don't think even that would make me feel better.

"Asshole! Get off me!" Her voice is high pitched, distressed, which makes my gut twist. And the tears cascading from her big, pretty hazel eyes make me want to fall to my knees and grovel for forgiveness.

The band director, Mrs. Williams, trots over.

"Oh, Zelda, you're bleeding. Beth, take her to the nurse. I'll get her stuff."

Beth nods and leads Zelda back through the gym doors, casting another year-stealing glare at me over her shoulder.

"Daniel," Mrs. Williams says in that tone of voice that preempts a future detention.

I hold my hands up in surrender. "It was a total accident, I promise, ma'am."

She nods. "All right, I'll believe you this time, but if any further harm comes to my first-string tuba player—"

"I would never hurt her or anyone on purpose, seriously. Do you think she'll be okay? I didn't break her nose, did I?"

She puts a hand on my shoulder. "I think she'll be fine. It didn't seem that bad."

I look around at the other band members. One of them had to have seen what really happened, right? But none of them will make eye contact with me. I know Zelda hates me because of that stupid thing I did a while back, the memory of which is safely tucked away in the good ol' guilt mind vault, but I didn't think she'd actively try to turn people against me. But that seems to be the case. Maybe I'm being paranoid, but I know her all too well. She's a grudge-holder and conniving, a deadly combination, and she's stated on many occasions that she would make my life a living hell. No telling what kind of monster she's painted me to be with these guys. And the funny/highly annoying thing is that if the universe were predictable, I'd be among them right now instead of wearing these stupid, ridiculously expensive basketball sneakers. Not that I have any idea how to play an instrument, but maybe I'd be hanging around, waiting for a friend to get done so I can give her a ride home. Maybe that friend would've been Zelda and we'd be currently trading good-natured insults. I'd say how silly she looked with her monster tuba and she'd say how I didn't need anything to look ridiculous because that's just my normal state of being. But the universe is not predictable, nor is it fair.

The band members don't owe me any kind of loyalty, though. I know that. Donovan, on the other hand, could've at least backed me up instead of, well, being himself. I try to keep the rising anger under control as I enter the locker room. I also try to emulate Beth's glare on Donovan, but it has no effect.

"Why can't they go prance around on the field like normal?" He tosses his jersey into his locker. "I mean, our practice is more important anyway, am I right? A little rain won't kill them."

"Why did you do that, dude?" I ask him, barely containing my rage.

He scoffs. "Do what?"

"Say that to Zelda? It was an accident. You're supposed to back me up. Team loyalty and all that crap."

He makes a *pfft* sound. "Whatever, man. Don't try to blame anything on me. You're the one who clocked her. But let's face it, a basketball to the nose could only be an improvement for her, am I right?" He turns to Lackey #1, hand raised for a high five.

I open my mouth to inform him that he'd be the luckiest d-bag on Earth if Zelda Potts ever even deigned to give him the time of day. I want to explain in very small, simple words so he will understand that she's so far out of his league the distance could only be measured in light years.

I've never wanted to deck someone so much, but I close my mouth and take a deep breath instead. That would be sinking to their level, as well as a waste of my time, since there's no changing people like Donovan. And if it's revenge I want, I can do better, I'm sure. I'm more concerned with what state Zelda is in anyway. What if her nose is broken? What if she got a black eye?

I'm quick to get dressed so I can head over to the nurse's office.

Zelda

"Honey, do you ever *not* get hurt at school?" Miss Carrie, the school nurse, asks as she cleans my face.

"I think you know the answer to that. Have you given any thought to my 'frequent visitor card' idea? By this point, I'm sure I could've earned a free Snoopy Band-Aid or something."

Miss Carrie laughs. "You've got it, dear. I have some in my drawer. It doesn't look like anything is broken, so that's good. Just a little bloody nose. It'll be sore and red for a while."

I start humming "Rudolph the Red-Nosed Reindeer." Being a magnet for accidents has taught me one thing, at least: all you can do is laugh it off. But this time it wasn't an accident, was it? It was someone's fault. Not just any someone's, but Dan Garrett's. And it wasn't something small like a stubbed toe; it was a raging bloody nose in front of a gym full of people.

If it had been anyone else, it would be easy for me to brush it off. Okay, maybe not "easy" because that sucked really hard. But it was Dan-freaking-Garrett, which makes it suck a million times worse. He's been on my shitlist ever since he ditched me to go to some party a while back. He was supposed to be at the LARP game with me, help me learn the ropes, but he decided to go hang with the "cool kids" or whatever they're called. From that point on, it's just been one asshat incident after another. The bumping into me and not apologizing, the borrowing a pen and not giving it back. This one time he completely spaced on my name. Miss Pleasant paired us up to work on some questions addressing the current long, boring, old, dry tome we were reading in Advanced English.

"Dan, you can just sit back there by your partner. Please remember to stick to the topic," she said, acknowledging our propensities to veer off into the bigger picture and to bicker. The bickering is never-ending.

This was a few months ago, so he was riding the peak of his popular-dom, which he is still doing. He plopped down in the desk that is normally warmed by Beth and said, "Right, let's do this." Then he looked into my face and he went blank. Blank in every way possible. His face lost all animation and his hands went limp as he dropped his books onto the desk. Even his ass seemed to lose its way because he almost missed his seat entirely.

I remember rolling my eyes at him and opening my book. "Just try not to focus on three-pointers while we do this, okay? I, unlike most of the people you congregate with, am trying to actually make decent grades."

He laughed uncomfortably then. Such a sweet sound (sweet to my ears because he obviously felt so very out of his element). "Of course, Zetty, Prelda... You got it."

Then the arguing started. He never fails to say something that drives me crazy. He does it on purpose, I just know it. God forbid he's ever nice to me. If that does happen, you better start stockpiling canned goods and practicing your crossbow skills because the zombie apocalypse has occurred.

The sad thing is, I thought I'd come to terms with who Dan really is. I'd let go of any possibility of us being friends, or anything else. I was happy to deem him "just someone I used to know." I'd even gotten to the point where if I looked at him I didn't feel an angry cthulhu monster wrap its tentacles around the hostility sector of my brain. Then he had to go and do this.

We were so close for so long. We shared opinions, thoughts, and conjectures on the universe. Hell, I even talked to him about my view on sex. Granted, that took place a while ago, but my view hasn't changed. And what he did with that information is abominable. For someone who used to bitch about the inanity of popularity, he sure was quick to embrace it. It wasn't even a gradual change. One day, he was excited about LARPing and choosing which Sonic Screwdriver to buy, the next he was bro-hugging his fellow teammates and pretending like he had no idea how to do algebra because, "When are we ever going to need to know how to do this crap?" Probably every day for the rest of your life, Dan, or that's what you *used to say.*

Beth pokes her blond head in the door. "Doing okay?"

I nod just before Miss Carrie slaps an ice pack onto my face. I lay back and stare at the ceiling. It's one of those where they used putty to make a texture. I've spent many an afternoon analyzing this ceiling. It usually calms me down, as I try to find images in the random way the putty was smeared onto it. There's a gnome holding a balloon right there in the center. Over by the wall above the window is the profile of a woman crying. But my usual favorites seem to be turning on me. The gnome morphs into Dan's stupid, smug face in my head. He palms a basketball with a look of glee. Of course he'd ruin this simple little relaxation ritual for me.

He has seriously messed up this time. I'm not going to let this go unpunished. He's unleashed the tiger, heaven help him.

The problem, I quickly realize, is that Dan is smart, even if he pretends to be otherwise. He wouldn't fall for most of my dastardly plans like, say, Greg Donovan would. Dan Garrett would know what was going on. I have to think of something truly cunning, something inventive, if I want to remind him that he was once just like us. Just like me: a lowly nerd trying to navigate high school without losing my mind.

Miss Carrie finally releases me, so Beth and I head out of the empty school to her car. Poor Beth tries to cheer me up with small talk, but I'm having none of it.

"He stopped by, ya know?"

"Who?" I ask.

"Dan. Wanted to check on you."

Check on me? Yeah, right. He just wanted to see what he'd wrought. Like a murderer returning to the scene of the crime.

"But I was a good guardian." She puts on her atrocious British accent. "Sent 'im on his merry way, I did." She looks at me expectantly because she knows her British accent always makes me giggle. It's a testament to how pissed I am that I don't laugh.

"Thanks. He was probably just coming around to gloat, the jerkface." I pull on the car door handle, trying to punctuate my sentence with an angry gesture, but it's locked.

"Jerkface?" A voice comes from the other side of the vehicle parked in front of Beth's. I should have realized whose it was, but I was too busy focusing on the throbbing in my nose, I guess.

Dan walks around to the back of his enormous, hideously overpriced truck/Range Rover thing. "That's a colorful description. I kind of like it. It's a little juvenile, though. I'm sure you can do better, Zelda." His weirdly perfect lips quirk up on the right, causing smile wrinkles by his eyes. I mean, seriously, who has smile wrinkles at seventeen years old? Then he cocks his head to the right in a silent challenge.

The logical part of my brain is screaming for me to ignore him because if I take the bait, I'll set myself on a path of never-ending annoyance that will last until well into the early morning hours. But the pissed-off, just-got-clocked-with-a-basketball part of my brain wrestles Miss Logical Brain to the floor.

Challenge accepted, sir. "How about douche canoe? Assbutt? Bane of my existence? Sign of the imminent apocalypse? How do those work for you?" I pull on the car door handle again and, blessedly, it opens. I get in without giving him a chance to respond with some charming insult because I know that's his mode of operation: being a jerk to a person without that person even realizing it until later when she's in the shower or something, going over the conversation. Did you know squeezing the shampoo bottle in a fit of newly realized rage causes it to squirt quickly and directly into one's eyes? Well, it does, speaking from experience.

Beth gets in, cranks the car, and we're off, leaving Dan-the-Bland in the rearview mirror. Damn it, I should've used that one.

Beth puts on that British accent again. "Well, you showed 'im. Ee's such a twat."

I give her a noncommittal shrug and stare out the window.

She accepts defeat after that. If the accent won't work after being utilized *twice*, there's nothing that can be done for my mood. She drops me off at my house, throwing a "Hope you feel better" out the window as she pulls away. After a nice, long shower and a surprisingly short conversation with Mom during which she barely acknowledges my swollen nose—not because she doesn't care but because, well, this is me we're talking about—I settle down in front of the only thing that really understands me: my laptop. Tumblr is on fire tonight because of a short trailer that was released for *The Super Ones* movie. I try to switch on fangirl mode, but I'm still pissed about Dan. I shouldn't be, I know. I shouldn't let him get to me, but, dear Lord, how he gets to me! We used to be friends. He got me into LARPing, for goodness sake.

I'll admit, I had a slight crush on him back then, before he slimmed down and grew a few inches. I know quite a few girls who have a crush on him now. I've heard them in the halls or the bathroom, always discussing his dreamy eyes and luscious hair. Luscious. Oh, how I hate that word. But if I'm honest, there's no better word for it. It's got a slight wave to it and it's a honeyed brown. "Dreamy" is a good descriptor for his eyes, too. Bedroom eyes, concerned eyes with an edge of calculation. But those are both things he had before. I noticed them first, along with the other more important things. For example, once upon a midnight nerdy, we had a cult horror movie marathon. We stayed up until the wee hours of the morning wallowing in the epic awesomeness of Johnny Depp in *Nightmare on Elm Street,* the ultimate creep-level of Pennywise the clown in the *IT* mini-series, and the always present stupidity of girls in most scary movies.

"It's a shame, really," he'd said that night, nodding to the screen. "Here's an opportunity for Hollywood to show feminine strength and what does she do? She hides under the bed." He shook his head and munched on a cheesy puff.

I got a wiggly feeling in my stomach. "My thoughts exactly." There's nothing sexier than a guy who believes girls are actual people with intelligence and worth. I guess, for some weird reason, that's why I find his nerdom betrayal so horrific. He had so much potential and he let popularity dig its professionally manicured claws into him.

Again, my thoughts go back to getting even with him. And suddenly it hits me. What's the best way to defeat a foe? Know thy enemy.

Oh yes, Google will be my friend.

The first few results when I Google Dan Garrett are pretty standard. There's a mention in the *Natchitoches Times* about the basketball team getting to the finals. There's Dan's long-abandoned LiveJournal page, which boasts a very whiny, horribly written poem. I tuck that away for later. And there's a mention of him in an interview with his dad, who's a local celebrity known as "Taxidermy Todd." I don't even click on that because everyone knows everything about Taxidermy Todd. He's the hometown boy who made it big a few years ago by being one of the nation's leading taxidermists. He even starred in a reality show on TLC. It was just a pilot episode— the series didn't get picked up—but it was the biggest thing to happen to Natchitoches since *Steel Magnolias* was filmed here. And it boosted Mr. Garrett's business so much that he doesn't even need to do it anymore. He's still involved in it, goes to conventions, speaks with up-and-coming taxidermists, that kind of thing, but no more preserving poor, beautiful animals some rich asshole shot on safari. He might do a favor for someone like Old Lady So-and-So who lost her beloved, so-old-it-was-blind-and-deaf cat, but other than that, he's done.

It's toward the bottom of the page that I find pure gold.

Oh yes, Dan Garrett needs to be taught a lesson, and school is in session.

Chapter Two
DAN

Maddie rolls her eyes so hard they probably have a fantastic view of her frontal lobe. "Dan, are you seriously complaining about being popular?"

I should've known better than to say anything to her. She doesn't understand. "Well, I—"

She straightens the comics in the H-section of The Phoenix as she bitches me out. "I mean, you do realize there are people with far worse problems than being popular, right? Some people have to walk five miles just to get water every day. Some people don't know how to read. Jeez, some people *died* today."

"Yeah, I understand that and I'm sorry for their pain, but… Never mind. Forget it. Excuse the hell out of me for thinking you might actually be able to help me with something, that I could actually confide in you without my balls being busted." I turn to leave her to her OCD ways.

She stops me by putting a hand on my shoulder. "Wait, wait, wait. I'm sorry, okay? Of course you can confide in me. Let's start over. So, why don't you like being popular?"

I give her an "I don't quite trust you, but I'm going to give it a shot" eye squint because if anyone knows about being in the "It crowd," it's Maddie. She spent most of her high school years around these people. "I don't know. I guess I just don't believe in the concept. It's like, who gives a flying rat's ass what people think of you, ya know? Their approval isn't going to do anything for you in the future. Unless they're, like, Bill Gates's nephew or something and you want to build computers or robots who wash your socks. Man, wouldn't it be great to have a robot sock-washer?"

"Uh, hasn't that already been invented?" She taps a finger on her chin in fake thought. "Oh yeah! It's called a washing machine."

"Ha. Ha. Ha. Very funny, cheerleader."

She takes a dramatic bow. "Thank you! You've been a wonderful crowd. I'm here all week, tell your friends."

I scoff. "Yeah, sure."

"What is it with you and socks anyway? It's like you're obsessed or something."

I shake my head in pity for her tiny, tiny brain. "The right socks are like a hug for your feet that lasts all day. It's the little things that make life bearable."

"Weirdo," she says, then looks out the front window dreamily. "Seriously though, I'd prefer a robot homework-doer. I have like three papers due next week. And they're all for classes where the professors are meanies."

And there's the college talk. It's all Maddie and her boyfriend/my hetero life partner Logan discuss now. That and each other. A couple of years ago, all kinds of stupid drama-rama went down between them. They started out as star-crossed lovers with her being the quintessential popular cheerleader and him being the king of the nerds. But I took it upon myself to make sure those two crazy kids lived happily-ever-after and all that other junk. The number of times I've seen them do that cute, cuddly, kissy stuff is truly appalling. I'm not jealous at all… Okay, maybe a little. Or a lot. But it's still gross to see, since I think of them both more like siblings now.

Normally, I'd just be bored by the college talk, but at the moment, it's another topic that goes into the "things I'm jealous of" category. It must be heaven to be out of high school. "And by meanies, you really mean that they don't fall for your made-up excuses, right?"

She sticks her tongue out at me and we make our way to the checkout counter of the store. "Anyway, what specifically don't you like about having people like you?"

I shrug. "It's such a hassle. I have to be, like, *nice* to them. It makes me very uncomfortable, as you could imagine." She nods in the affirmative as I continue. "And it's not just my aversion to being nice to people, ya know? It comes with responsibilities and obligations I just don't want or need in my life. Plus, these people, dude, they're straight-up horrible."

She laughs. "I can see how that would make you, Craytor of the 'every-dwarf-for-himself' clan, uncomfortable. You're not exactly a people person. And I knew my share of the holier-than-thou crowd, so I get that."

I can't hold in a long sigh. Craytor, my poor LARP (which stands for live action roleplaying for those who aren't cool enough to know) character. I had such big plans for him this year, but I have no time to even go to the games. Not to mention my dad has strictly forbidden anything and everything game related. Come to think of it, he's kind of forbidden everything that gives me joy. It has a lot to do with him wanting me to be the best I can be, to get into a good college and be friends with the "right people," whatever that means. But that's a pity party for another day. Right now I'm more depressed over the fact that even Maddie's little elf princess thing could take on Craytor because I've missed out on a butt-ton of experience points that I could've used to make him even more badass.

I give one of the shelves a good kick. "Don't even bring up LARP of Ages. It makes my heart hurt."

"Sorry." She pats me on the back, completely serious. Even despite their college workload, both Maddie and Logan have been able to make it to every game. "So what are you going to do? If it makes you this miserable, you should remedy the situation, right?"

I run my fingers through my hair, which always

makes it stick up a little. "You think I haven't tried? I thought if I was a jerk, maybe all these cheerleaders and football players and cool kids and other stereotypes would stop asking me to hang out and stuff, but it's like that makes them want to hang out with me more. What sort of messed-up world do they live in, dude? And sometimes…" I shake a finger at her so she realizes the severity of what I'm about to say. "Sometimes, they just show up at my house."

Her eyes go wide. "Noooo…"

"Yes."

"You don't let them into your inner sanctum, do you?"

That question goes to show how well this simple former cheerleader has gotten to know me.

"Of course I don't let them into my room. There are too many valuable treasures in there. Could you imagine if one of those muscle-heads were to pick up my limited-edition Mace Windu lightsaber? He'd probably crush it with his big, meaty paws. No, they do not come into the inner sanctum. I usually just give them a towel and point them in the direction of the pool."

She lets out a relieved sigh. "Phew, thank goodness. I might start to feel pushed aside if you let someone other than me in there."

"You're only allowed because of the 'friend's girlfriend' clause, so don't go and get a big head about it."

Her mouth drops open in a mock-offended manner and her hand covers her heart. "You wound me, sir."

I wave off her dramatics. "Anyway. What am I supposed to do?"

"Sounds like you're just going to have to grin and bear it." She shakes her head, her blond ponytail, which now features a streak of hot pink, swinging back and forth.

"Well, aren't you just super helpful. Oh wait, did you hear that?" I hold my hand up, listening.

She frowns at me. "Hear what?"

"That severe note of sarcasm in my voice. Because you're *not* being helpful at all. Let's be honest here, you're like the expert on identity crises, so where are the pearls of wisdom? Where are the nuggets of simple yet strangely accurate advice?" I grab a stack of comics that need to be shelved. Maybe if I help her get work done, she'll be more inclined to take me seriously.

"But is this really an identity crisis? You of all people know who you are, in my opinion. Why don't you just tell all these guys to leave you alone?

I mean, I don't really advise it because that would be mean, but that sounds like something you'd do."

I pause in the middle of straightening the *Batgirl* comics because she makes a good point. *Why am I indulging them?* I ask myself. Immediately, an image of my dad's satisfied face pops into my head. He looked so happy when Douchebag Donovan showed up with at least ten other people in tow for a surprise pool party. I don't mention this to Maddie, though, because I know what she'd say. It'd be something Confucius-like that doesn't help me fix my main problem at all. "You can't live your life for someone else," or some such lame thing that's easier said than done.

In the end, I just tell her I'm probably overreacting and change the subject because my brain is tired of thinking about important stuff and not getting anywhere. It's much more at home thinking about which new title to add to my pull list.

Zelda

Ah, Sundays. The best day of the week. Sundays have been dubbed cosplay day by Beth and me. We've decided to go out on a limb and create costumes for *The Super Ones* midnight premier at the theater. This will be the first film based on the über-popular comic book series, so we want to do it up right. We both wanted to be Bright Frenzy, the main mammajamma, but Beth made a very good argument with the fact that she's taller than me by a couple of inches and BF *is* one of those floaty, willowy types. I'm cool with being Frenzy's awesome sidekick Finity Girl, since I 'ship her and the Young One so hard.

We've been doing tons of research online on how to make capes and realistic-looking armor. Finity Girl has this short, satiny black cape and shiny black armor. Plus, I've already bought a blond wig that's perfect.

I plop the fabric for my cape on Beth's dining room table then pull out my laptop from its bag. Beth's older sister, Cara, has given in to helping us with the sewing, since she's a fashion design major. She's this ultra-chic, homemade-clothes-wearing woman, and I kind of have a lady crush on her. She "customized" her sewing machine by using different colored duct-tape to create all these geometric shapes. It's a freaking work of art.

She plugs in her masterpiece. "Did you find

some reference images, Zelda?"

"So many, it's ridiculous. I mean, some of them aren't canon, ya know, from the comic or whatever. They're fan-made, but I like them." I pull up my bookmark folder for all my Finity Girl pictures.

She leans over my shoulder to see the screen of my laptop. "That's cool, though. We could work in some of the little things you like."

I grin. This chick so gets me, but it'd probably be weird if I asked her to be my best friend forever, right?

Beth comes into the dining room lugging tons of fabric and supplies. "Do you think we'll be able to get the capes finished today? I'm not ashamed to admit that I want to wear mine on a daily basis."

Cara laughs. "Shouldn't be too hard to get them done."

Beth does a fist pump. "Yes!"

"On one condition, though," Cara says.

Beth goes from petting the smooth fabric to clutching it. "What?" she asks suspiciously.

Cara puts her fists on her hips. "You have to promise me you'll decide this upcoming week which colleges to apply to. And then actually *apply* to them when the time comes."

Beth lets out a long sigh. "I'll look into colleges,

but I'm not promising anything. I might need to take a break after high school. Live a little, ya know."

Cara scrunches up her nose and light reflects off her Monroe piercing. "Fine, but you need to start thinking about this stuff."

I get a twinge of jealousy at this conversation. It must be nice to basically have your pick of colleges. I'll be lucky if I get any kind of help with tuition. It's not that I'm not smart. I just don't think I'm *that* smart. Writing all those essays for grants and scholarships would be beyond me. But none of that even matters because I have no idea what I want to do with my life. There are only a few jobs that are in the "Definite No" column for me.

My mental image of my future self is pretty vague. I know I want to help people somehow. Better the world and all that. But how am I supposed to make such an important decision at this point in my life? I know if I do go to college, it'll be a one-shot deal. I don't want to spend years learning something I eventually realize isn't the right thing for me, so I'll have to get it right the first time. I've heard too many horror stories about the mountains of financial aid debt a person can build up. I don't want to be that person.

I don't know. Indecision sucks. Time for a

change of subject.

As Cara threads her machine, I motion for Beth to come over and look at my computer. "Remember how I said I'd get Dan? Well, I found something the other night."

Her brows knit when she looks at the website I've opened. "Dan's Tumblr page? I didn't know he had a Tumblr. But what does that have to do with anything?"

"Don't you see? I have a way to mess with him now. And he'll never know it's me. I'm going to set up a fake page and let the games begin."

"So, you're going to anonymously call him names or something?" She looks taken aback.

"No, that's troll behavior and cowardly. My plan is a lot more long term and involved than that."

Beth's quiet for a moment as she stares at the ceiling, gears turning. Then she makes a face like the lightbulb just clicked on in her head. "Oh, I get it! Wait… Nope, I don't get it."

"You'll see. Just wait. Just wait…"

"You have no idea what you're going to do, do you?"

"Oh, ye of little faith. I was thinking last night that I have to get him to trust me somehow, to the point where he'll tell me anything. Then I'd worm some piece of dirt out of him. Everyone has a deep, dark secret, and everyone has a weird desire to reveal that secret. But then it occurred to me as I was daydreaming about embarrassing the hell out of Dan that I was being very selfish. That even if I got my revenge on him, what good would it actually do? Other than give me immense pleasure and satisfaction and make me feel like the lady in *The Help* who made the poo-pie? I have an opportunity here and the will to carry it out."

"Carry what out?" Beth asks as she waves a piece of fabric in the air to test its, as she calls it, flowy factor.

I pull up Blogspot on my computer and start the process of creating a new page. "A human social behavior experiment. The first of its kind, dude."

Cara turns to me. "A what now?"

"I've known Dan for years. We were really close friends once upon a time, then all of a sudden, WHAM!" I smack my hands together to give the full effect. "He goes from Mister Nobody to the king of the scene. And all because he's good at basketball and he became pretty close to the definition of 'attractive.' What kind of world do we live in, y'all, when all it takes is a good three-pointer and nice eyes to become everyone's favorite person? Anyway, I've always found the concept of 'popularity' a strange one, and this is my chance to understand it. Why are some people popular and others not? What does it do to a person? What does it do for society in general?"

Beth's brows knit together. "So, you're going to, what, study him? Basically use him as a guinea pig?"

"Exactly. The whole thing will be in the name of science so, ya know, I'm not tricking him or anything. I'm doing this for the good of society. Plus, he'll never know. My blog will be totally anonymous." I don't mention that I'm looking forward to it in a weird, sadistic way because that would not paint me in a good light.

Cara snorts and points a finger at me. "Just tread carefully, okay?"

"Don't worry," I assure her, "I've got this."

Beth and Cara begin to discuss how to make sure our costumes have just enough va-va-voom without having to use double-sided tape on our boobs, and my mind wanders. It settles comfortably into guilt mode.

Am I a horrible person for doing this to Dan? Probably. Should I forget the whole thing? Double probably. Will I? Probably not, because the second

I start to think about the bad thing I'm trying to do to him, I remember the bad things he's done to me. The basketball incident is just the final drop in the bucket. He doesn't know it, but I heard him that day almost a year ago talking to his "friends" in the locker room. I never thought the air conditioning being broken in the boys' locker room would be a fortuitous thing for me.

The door was propped open so they could get a little air flow in there and Martin Hedge's voice floated into the hall, along with some pretty foul odors, I might add. "What about that Zelda girl?"

"No, man," Dan said, "she's not like the others. There's no satisfaction to be had there."

It's said that smell is the sense that most easily evokes memories. B.O. and sweaty sneakers will forever remind me of the day Dan Garrett truly became a jerkwad in my book. I'd been holding out hope up to that very moment that Dan wasn't a total shithead, but I couldn't live in denial anymore. He was just like the rest of them, concerned about one thing and one thing only: getting laid. And yes, I know hormones are a thing that happens to guys, because they happen to girls, too. And yes, I've also spent some time talking about the sexual appeal of this or that guy with Beth, but it was never in a disrespectful way. Dan took something I told him in confidence and twisted it, made it sound like the fact that I wouldn't put out meant that I wasn't worth the time. And *that* is a big ol' bucket full of nope.

We'll be even stevens after this. He might never know it, but I will, and that's what matters. Yeah, I'll go with that. I'm doing this for the good of humanity, for science. My conscience is clear.

Chapter Three
DAN

"Coach, forgive me, but how does riding the bus to games instead of taking my comfortable vehicle give me life experience?" I lean forward and hook an arm over the back of Coach's seat so I can see his face.

His expression doesn't read, "What an interesting and well-articulated question, Daniel," like I was hoping it would. It reads more like, "If you don't shut the hell up, I'll *give* you some real-life experience."

I smile and sit back. "Never mind."

Before I kill some time with a little Angry

Birds on my phone, I check the notifications I've gotten from my blog. Looks like someone really enjoys my posts. There are "likes" and "reblogs" all over the place. Her name is effyeahFinityGirl and her picture is… Well, it's mysterious, I guess. I can't really see her face. Her long blond hair obscures her profile, but I can make out a heart-shaped mouth. And she's sent me a message.

> **effyeahFinityGirl:** Hi, Dantheman! Just wanted to let you know that I absolutely love your blog! I'm a big Super Ones fan, too! Although the new spin-off is slightly unoriginal, I'm hopeful it'll get better. Would love to chat about it if you're up for it?

Okay, so she overuses exclamation points, but wow, talk about a girl after my own heart. I got into a heated debate with Logan just the other day about the unoriginality of the Super Ones spin-off.

> **Me:** Finally, someone with some sense! Are you free later? I'd love to have an intelligent conversation about the spin-off with someone who isn't easily swayed by sentimentality like most of my friends.

I check back over the message. Led with a

compliment? Check. Big words? Check. Friendliness? Check. I think there's a certain finesse to talking with strangers on the internet. Especially potentially hot strangers.

Message sent.

After a few fails at Angry Birds level thirty-two and a shouting match with Douchebag Donovan about him kicking the back of my seat, my phone dings with a new message from effyeahFinityGirl.

> **effyeahFinityGirl:** I'm definitely free later! I'm a night owl so I'll be up for a while. Just message me. Sound good?

Score. I swear, talking to girls online is so much easier than in real life. In real life, there's body language and tone of voice to consider. I just don't have the attention span to be able to focus on whether or not a flip of the hair is flirting or batting away a fly. Of course, this could be a thirty-year-old man, but whatever. It's not like I'll ever actually meet this person.

Talk to you then, I message her just as we're pulling into the Lakeview School's parking lot.

We all pile out of the bus and head to the locker room. I freaking hate away games. I think it all boils down to the smell. The smell of some other place's locker rooms and court is always different. Not to mention that feeling of "we all hate you here."

We suit up. Everyone is quiet like they always are before a game. Getting in the zone and all that. Like the others, I have my own way of revving up. I have this playlist on my phone full of nothing but music from movies. Particularly the songs that were playing during the "workout montages." Nothing beats "Eye of the Tiger" when you're getting ready to demolish the other team.

The band is setting up in the bleachers when we head onto the court for the pre-game warm-up. It's hard not to find Zelda because of that bright red hair, even if it's almost all covered by that goofy feather hat. I still feel the need to talk to her about what happened at practice the other day. I tried to get in to see her when she was in the nurse's office, but Beth was guarding the door like a Roman soldier. And that scene in the parking lot did not go like I wanted it to. When I catch Zelda's attention, she doesn't give me the Eye of Hate as I was expecting. She's smiling. Which, at first, makes me think, *Great, she's not pissed*, but then I realize how weird it is. The girl hasn't smiled at me since I bailed on that one LARP game. I still kind of feel bad about that. Craytor, my badass dwarf, was supposed to mentor her new dwarf character, but I got invited to a party that night. This was during my make-the-cool-kids-hate-me phase in which I acted like an idiot at their parties in the hopes they wouldn't want anything more to do with me. Of course, the more stupid and immature I acted, the more they wanted me around.

I raise an eyebrow at her, a big, silent "What are you up to?" written across my face, I'm sure.

She just smiles bigger and goes back to talking with Beth. I look around me, wondering if maybe that smile was meant for someone else, but it's just me.

I don't like this. Not one bit. Zelda is definitely one of the smartest chicks I've ever met. She's also one of the most stubborn. So, why the smile when she's supposed to hate me?

A bad feeling creeps across the back of my neck when she looks at me again, that smile still in place. Don't get me wrong, it's a great smile. I've always thought she was adorable. I thought so even more after I lost her. It's like that quote: Absence makes the heart feel like a microwaved burrito, never quite warm in the middle and burn-your-tongue hot on the outside.

I'm about to charge up the bleachers to find out what her deal is, but I feel a hand on my shoulder. I turn and come face-to-face with Carrie Danvers, one of our cheerleaders. She's been pursuing me pretty hardcore for the past couple of weeks. It's hard for me to keep in an exasperated sigh.

"Hey, Dan. You going to the after party tonight?" She bats her heavily mascaraed eyes.

"Uh… Nah, I've got plans."

She nudges me with her shoulder. "Aw, come on. I'll be there."

"Sorry, I can't. I have a date…thing," I say, hoping it'll throw her off my trail.

Wishful thinking, Dan. "Well, if you get bored on your date thing, text me." She licks her lips and sorta bites the bottom one. The action is so deliberately over-the-top.

I grunt as a response, then escape to our team's seats. Douchebag Donovan plops down next to me and something is off. Normally, he's a ball of nervous energy at this point. I learned early on not to stay too close to him before a game because he gets weirdly yell-y and headbutt-y, like a good concussion is what the team needs to be revved up and win or something. But right now, he just slumps down in his chair with his bottom lip poking out like a scolded child.

It takes me a minute to decide whether or not to leave him alone. In the end, my better nature takes control. "Dude? You okay?"

"Mind your own business, Garrett." He shoots eye-daggers across the gym at his dad, who is finding a place to sit, and it doesn't take a genius to figure out he's having some type of parental discord.

"Yeah," I say, "my dad's kind of an asshole, too."

He jumps to his feet, fists at the ready and eye-daggers now targeting me. "You calling my dad an asshole?" He's like a mountain of rage, and I do not want to be a casualty of that avalanche.

I hold my hands up and scoot back a little in my chair. "No, dude. Not at all. I'm sure he's a fine, upstanding gentleman."

His stance relaxes and he sits down again. "That's what I thought."

That's when I notice the red mark on his cheek. I think about maybe addressing it, but the ref blows his whistle, signifying the start of the game.

Zelda

"Well, that was like shooting fish in a barrel, wasn't it?" Beth asks as we unpack our instruments.

"I told you. This is going to be so epic. He has no idea what's about to hit him. I mean, science has no idea what's about to hit it."

"Uh huh," she says in that way of hers that means I'm not fooling her for a second. "So what's going to happen on this date?" She cuts her eyes at me mischievously.

I scoff. "Date? No. No, this is not a date. This is experiment A."

"Not a date? Okay, number one, you've set a time to meet. You're meeting in a chat room, but it still counts. Two, y'all will be talking for an extended period of time about things you both find interesting. This is so a date, Zelda."

"Fine. But it's a fake date. It's not like I have any amorous feelings for him or anything."

"You used to, though. Remember?"

I scowl at her, then look around to make sure no one is listening to us. If someone were to hear even an implication that I used to have a thing for Dan,

I'd be mortified. "Don't you even. That was forever ago, and he's not the same person he was then. That Dan didn't ignore friends. That Dan didn't lie about having something super important to do then go to a party on a Saturday night instead of LARPing. That Dan didn't objectify me to his new friends. It's all just…Just. Unforgivable." I make sure there's not even a hint of humor in my next words. "And if you suggest there's anything going on between us again, I will be forced to hurt you. Not even joking, okay?"

Her eyes go wide and she holds her hands up in surrender. "Okay, okay. Note taken. I have to admit he did pull a one-eighty when he started playing basketball. I never in a million years would have expected him to go to one of those parties."

"Exactly. I mean, look at him." Just as if he heard my words, which is impossible because he's down on the court and we're up in the bleachers, Dan turns his head in my direction.

Our eyes connect. If this would have happened a couple of days ago, I would've just given him the Eye of Hate and looked away. But I'm feeling super-confident at the moment, so I meet his gaze full on. I even smile a little. *I've got you now, you traitor.*

"Oh, I don't mind admitting that I do look at

him. Frequently. He's pretty hot." Beth giggles.

I break eye contact with Dan to stare dumbfounded at Beth. "What is wrong with you? He's not even close to being hot. I mean, sure, he does have nice hair, but external beauty isn't everything. In fact, it doesn't mean much at all, in my opinion."

"You're kidding, right? He's like if a young Bob Dylan and James Dean had a baby."

I shake my head. "Again, none of that matters. He's a jerk."

"Whatever you say, Miss 'How can anyone hate Justin Bieber? He's so gorgeous.'"

I punch Beth playfully in the shoulder. "I'm never going to live down my Bieber phase, am I?"

"Nope."

The game starts and we take our cues from the conductor. Between playing the regular sports hits like "Another One Bites the Dust" and helping the cheerleaders with some chants, I watch the game. Even if I find most of the guys on the team repulsive, I can't stop myself from cheering them on. Dan isn't doing as well as he normally does though. He keeps tripping and stuff. Weird. But I refuse to feel bad for him. Instead I repeat the game plan I came up with last night, over and over in my head.

Introduce

Admire

Make conversation

Gain trust

Remain vigilant

Outsmart target

Obtain proof of hypothesis

Terminate contact

This plan is as solid as a hundred-year-old tree.

If this works out—no, *when* this works out— it'll be a blow to all those people in my school who think they're in any way better than someone else. I want to prove that popularity changes people for the worst. I want those aspiring to popularity to realize that it's not worth it. That it is, in fact, folly and can only lead to the decay of one's morals and self-worth.

Take Colin, the team's equipment manager, for instance. Right now he's busting his ass to keep the players hydrated and stocked with fresh, clean towels. But do they ever thank him? Do they ever deign to just give a nod of appreciation? Not that I've ever seen. Then why does he continue? Some might bright-side the answer and say he needs some extra-curriculars on his transcript. And to those some, I say, "Give me a break." He does it in the hopes of making popular friends. He does it in search of acceptance, and poor Colin will never get that. But what if he was better at sports, or he fit in with their preconceived ideas about physical beauty? He'd be a shoe-in. It's all about the surface layer with them, and I hate that.

This mission could turn into something big, a kind of screw-you to all those people who think the sun rises and sets with them. All I have to do is follow my simple plan to the letter and victory shall be mine.

Chapter Four
DAN

As expected, we crushed the aptly named Hornets. I say "aptly named" because crush is what I do to all winged, stinging things. They are pointless creatures, and all deserve to die. Except for bees—they're very important, but they can still leave me the hell alone, please.

My stupid new shoes didn't do me any favors during the game, though. Every time the rubber gripped the court too hard, I felt my cheeks heat up, and Donovan didn't help. I've never seen him so into a game before. As captain, it's partly his responsibility to keep our heads in the game, but tonight he was just...mean.

When I get home, I put my world back into order by using my own shower instead of the one at that weird-smelling school, then I sit down to my computer. I do the usual internet stuff like checking my social networks and watching a couple of videos that will most likely become the next viral sensations. Dad stops by my room before heading to bed. I have to beg to be able to stay up a little longer. It's humiliating. I think it's because we won tonight that he acquiesces.

At eleven on the dot, I message effyeahFinity-Girl with a quick, simple, "Hi." When she responds with her own "Hi," the conversation begins easily.

Me: So, tell me the truth, how did you feel about the death of Super Hedgehog?

This should tell me everything I need to know about this girl. The upcoming cinematic release of *The Super Ones* movie has rehashed the argument about the book's ending even though that happened almost two years ago. There are two schools of thought when it comes to the fact that Super Hedgehog was the only character to die in the final issue of *The Super Ones*. Some believe absolutely no one should have died. Some believe they cheapened the series by only killing off the animal. I'm firmly on the latter team.

> **effyeahFinityGirl:** I know what you're trying to do here. You're testing me, aren't you?

Ah, touché.

> **Me:** How do you mean "testing you"?

> **effyeahFinityGirl:** There's a big debate about this going on. I have a feeling that if I were to say that I hated it and that I think no one should have died and that "OMG how could they kill the hedgehog?!" you'd write me off as the proverbial "fake geekgirl." Amirite?

I squint at my screen. Okay, so she knows her stuff. I decide to go the honest route.

> **Me:** You got me. But you have to admit it's a valid question.

The little blinking "effyeahFinityGirl is typing…" flashes for a long time. Then a wall-o-text appears.

> **effyeahFinityGirl:** I agree. Totally valid. My answer? I don't think they should have killed the hedgehog. Not to preserve the quality of the series but because IT'S JUST NOT RIGHT! Super Hedgehog

just shouldn't have died. It made me cry, which was all it was meant to do. It had no bearing on the plot or on any character development. And, no, I didn't want anyone to die, but I probably would have been happier with everyone BUT Hedgehog dying, to be honest. Does that make me a "fake geekgirl"? Well, we probably shouldn't go into that because I believe there's no such thing as a "fake geekgirl." I do believe it makes me a compassionate person, though. Also, if you look at the series as a whole, it's still awesome. Just because you don't like the ending doesn't mean you should discount the entire thing, I think.

It takes me a while to form a response. On one hand, I want to rail against her. Of course the series was cheapened by this obvious ploy to make people tear up. The whole cliché was beneath the quality of writing we came to love about *The Super Ones*. On the other hand, she makes a valid argument. Just because I didn't like the ending doesn't mean I should dislike the entire series.

I must be taking too long to respond because she says:

effyeahFinityGirl: Are you regretting this chat already?

I'm very quick to answer.

Me: Of course not! This is the most interesting conversation I've had in forever.

I really mean that, too. I like to pretend that my opinion matters to people, but it really doesn't a lot of the time. Or at least, that's how it feels. In my true circle of friends, which is pretty small, I'm considered the resident nut job, the loud-mouthed, opinionated geek. Maybe it was all those years of being an immature know-it-all.

See, I have no illusions about how I'm thought of. I'm not upset about it, but it does make it hard to get people to take me seriously. So, to have this totally random girl validate my concerns and then not only call me out on my crap, but do it well, is exhilarating. I might just have to hang on to her.

Zelda

Dantheman: So, are you in high school?

Yes, this is exactly what I was hoping would happen. After a little nerd talk, his interest has been piqued, and now he's the first to ask about specifics. If I were to ask first, I might come across too strongly, and then he'd get suspicious.

Me: I might be. Are you?

I can't be too forthcoming with information, though, can't seem too eager. I have to ease him into my spider's web and make it seem like everything is his idea.

Dantheman: I am. A senior.

Me: Me too. So ready to be done with it all.

Dantheman: I know what you mean. I don't think there's anyone I'll miss.

He's not going to miss anyone? What a liar! What about all his cool hangers-on? What about all those "hot chicks" who are constantly giggling about him in their desks behind me?

Me: Really? You won't miss anyone?

Dantheman: Nope. Pretty much all my real friends have already graduated. And everyone else hates me or I hate them.

Ah, I see what he's doing now. He's trying to play the poor lonely-loner card. "I'm such a quiet, deep person. No one understands me. Only someone as compassionate and intelligent as you could heal my broken soul. Wanna meet and make out?" What a slime ball.

I want to tell him that I know exactly what he's up to, but that would put an end to my plan. Looks like I'm going to have to play his game.

Me: Aw, you poor thing. That's so sad.

Dantheman: *shrug* It's not that big of a deal really. What about you? How's school life other than being ready to get out of the hellhole they call the public education system?

I giggle a little at that, then firmly cut it out. No giggling. He is not funny. He is stupid and hypocritical, Zelda. Never identify with the bad guy. Unless it's Loki from *Thor*. Then identify the pants off of him.

Me: Not much to say, really. I have one good friend and that's all I need.

Dantheman: Just one? Why just one? You seem like a smart, funny, considerate person. Is there something about you that you're not telling me?

Me: Oh, you mean the thing about my conjoined twin? Must have left that out.

Dantheman: LOL!

Wow, an all caps lol? In my understanding of online conversation, that means he really did laugh out loud. A little pinprick of pride blossoms in my chest and I decide not to tamp it down. Why should I? A little ego boost never hurt anyone.

Me: Seriously, though, there just isn't anybody else at my school that I care to put any effort into, ya know?

Dantheman: Yeah, I know that feeling. I mean, there is one person, but I kind of blew it with her.

Ooooh, here we go. If I can get him gossiping, I can prove a piece of my hypothesis. A good person does not talk about people behind their backs. The old Dan would never have done that. Or what if he has a thing for someone's girlfriend? What if it's more scandalous than that? Like a teacher? Oh, the possibilities. Something like that would be an even better indicator of the toll popularity can take on a person's morals. But of course I can't come right out and ask who it is. I have to be sneaky. This is very sneaky business, after all.

Me: Why do you think you blew it?

Dantheman: I don't *think*, I *know*. It's a long story.

Damn it. It's too early in our online relationship to press him for more information. Time to earn his trust a bit more.

Me: Oh well. Nothing to do about it now, right? Anyway, are you excited for *The Super Ones* movie?

Dantheman: Am I excited? Does a bear spit in the woods?

Me: Uh. Number 1: I don't think that's the saying. And number 2: I don't even know if bears spit.

Dantheman: Of course bears spit. Everything spits.

Me: That's debatable.

Dantheman: Everything has saliva, right?

Me: That doesn't mean everything spits.

The conversation then devolved into defining the act of spitting versus the act of drooling, which then turned into trading YouTube videos of animals spitting/drooling. And despite my earlier promise to myself to not laugh at his jokes, our chat session is some of the funniest few hours of my life so far. Of course, this is a fact I will never admit to anyone else but myself. It's also an occurrence that I promise to never let happen again. How am I supposed to treat him as a guinea pig when that video he sent me of a llama spitting at a screaming grandma nearly makes me pee my pants?

Chapter Five
DAN

The next night, I decide to tackle film. EffyeahFinityGirl displayed her comic book knowledge last night, but I'm passionate not only about comics. Plus, I could use a little time to geek out with someone, since most of my social interactions only entail schoolwork or dodging innocuous flirting or counting out loud to no one in particular the amount of three pointers I hit in a row.

With a Mountain Dew in hand, along with a bowl of baby carrots so I don't feel too much like a horrible lying son (my dad has me on this awful diet that in no way includes Mountain Dew, but the

carrots make up for my transgression, I think), I
message effyeahFinityGirl.

> **Me:** Can I ask you a very important
> question?

After a few minutes, she responds, letting me
know that she has about as much to do during the
weekend as I do.

> **effyeahFinityGirl:** I love very important
> questions. Proceed.

> **Me:** How do you feel about the *Evil Dead*
> movies?

Again, the "effyeahFinityGirl is typing..."
blinks for a while, and I find myself thirsting for her
opinion.

> **effyeahFinityGirl:** *Evil Dead 2* was a
> masterpiece, obviously. Those movies are
> like no others. But then they had to go and
> wreck it. The remake held none of the campy
> humor that I loved about the originals. It
> makes me wonder whether or not Raimi
> really had anything to do with it. And if he
> did, were the originals supposed to be like
> the new one if he had it to do over again?
> Which calls into question the awesomeness
> we all loved about the originals.

Dear Lord, could this girl speak my mind any better?

Me: Well said, and I totally agree. Next question: who shot first? Han or Greedo?

She doesn't even hesitate.

effyeahFinityGirl: Han, end of story. Next question.

If I were keeping score of how many times this girl gave me super-awesome shivers, the "yes" column would be as long as the line for Hall H at San Diego Comic Con.

Me: What was the last midnight showing you went to?

effyeahFinityGirl: You're going to think less of me, but I must be honest.

Oh no, I knew the other shoe had to drop at some point. She couldn't be perfect.

effyeahFinityGirl: It was the Batman movie before the most recent one. I couldn't make it to the last one. And I hate myself every day because of it.

At this, I literally pet the screen. I was expecting something very much against my personal tastes, but in reality she's just sad because she had to claim Nerd Level 9 and couldn't meet Nerd Level 10. Is it too early to propose marriage or at least civil-online-union?

> **Me:** That's not so bad. I mean, it's horrible, you should be so ashamed of yourself, but not friendship-ending. And just to make you feel better, I'll reveal something, but you have to promise not to be too hard on me.

> **effyeahFinityGirl:** Oooh, reveal away!

> **Me:** I read the Lord of the Rings trilogy only after I'd seen the movies.

I'm waiting on pins and needles for her reply when Dad bangs on my door. I jump, almost knock over my Dew, and thank the heavens when I catch it before a drop is spilled. For some reason, I just know he'd be able to smell it through the door.

"Yeah," I say before he gets too testy and uses his key for my door. He might be similar to a drill sergeant, but Mom has impressed upon him a young man's need for privacy.

"Daniel, get in bed. Can't have your hours getting screwed up."

"Yes sir." I close my laptop because I know he's waiting and watching for the lights in my room to go out before he leaves. Only when I hear his footsteps heading back downstairs do I pull out my phone, get in bed, and scoot completely under the covers.

effyeahFinityGirl: ...I just... I can't... I don't think I'll ever see you the same again.

Me: Come on. You must know how drawn out and dry some of JRR's writing can be. It was taking me forever to get through those books.

effyeahFinityGirl: Point taken, but it's still unsettling.

I grin at my phone, or have I been grinning this whole time? I'm not sure.

Me: Next question, and this is kind of a big one. The debate has been ongoing between me and a couple of my friends for years. You ready?

effyeahFinityGirl: Hit me with it.

Me: Who would win in battle: Darth Vader or Lord Voldemort?

Zelda

It's like I'm waking up with a hangover every morning after I talk to Dan. I'm confused, so I repeat the events of last night and try to find the moment that things went blurry. At the start of the chats, I have a purpose, a set goal. Then halfway through I forget that purpose and just go with the flow. Talking to him is intoxicating.

If he could stop being so... so... I don't even know if there's a word in my vocabulary to describe how he's acting in these chats. He's actually interested in my opinions, in my life, and he never says one jerky comment like I'm used to him doing. And I hate him for it.

He just needs to stop.

How am I supposed to make any progress on my experiment when he distracts me by being nice to me? I know, he's being nice to the other me, but it's still, well, nice. I need to rally. I need to buckle down and focus on the goal.

Remember, Zelda, you long for justice. You do not think Dan Garrett is adorable in any way.

I slam my locker door and nod firmly to myself. When I turn, there's the object of my ire talking to one of his teammates by the library entrance. I suddenly feel like I'm in one of those costly movie shots where everything speeds up except for the main character who goes into slow-mo. I'm a badass anti-heroine on a mission. Channeling all my anger, I frown at him as I pass. He catches sight of me over the guy's shoulder, and his face scrunches up in confusion. *Nope, that sweetly idiotic expression won't work on me, Dan*, I say in my head, but then I make a huge mistake. I make complete eye contact with him and everything goes from slo-mo to not-moving-at-all. A tingle runs down my spine and stops in my stomach where it seems to bounce around, ping-ponging all over the place. My determination melts away and I grin. It's a familiar grin, the kind that happens when a gif of a hot guy holding a puppy pops up on my Tumblr feed. But it feels unfamiliar in these circumstances. In real life. Caused by and directed at *him*.

I don't know how long the grin lasts because of the time-standing-still thing. When I come to my senses, my eyes go wide and so does his smile. I take off like the coward I am.

I safely avoid Dan for the rest of the day, but

that doesn't stop me from thinking about him. Maybe "thinking" is the wrong word? It didn't stop me from being confused as hell about him. Yeah, that's more accurate.

After school, I ride with Beth over to the comic shop. My spirits lift when I see Maddie Summers behind the counter, reading a novel. I first met Maddie at one of the LARP of Ages games, but I first *knew* of her as one of the school's princesses of popularity. From what I understand, she was a nerd on the inside and felt the need to obtain popularity so she wouldn't be made fun of. I might think about mentioning her situation on my blog because, in my opinion, it's just more evidence of what this silly notion of popularity can do to a person's self-image.

"Welcome, ladies." She sticks her bookmark between the pages as we hop onto the counter. "What's the word, birds?"

"You wouldn't happen to have a black wig I could borrow, would you?" Beth asks.

Most people would be thrown off by the question, but most people do not traverse the LARPing or the cosplay world. Maddie doesn't bat an eye. "I don't think so, but I bet Logan's mom, Martha, does. I'll ask when she comes in."

"Awesome." Beth jumps into explaining about our costumes for *The Super Ones* midnight premier. "We've already gotten most of them done. You should see our capes. They're amazing. And Zelda looks perfect as Finity Girl."

Maddie slaps her hands on the counter. "I *love* Finity Girl! How hard did you cry when she rescued that little orphan girl in #16 of *The Bright Frenzy*?"

"Right?!" I clutch at my heart. "It was like she was rescuing herself, since there were so many similarities between them. And if you notice, in her room in #25, there's a bulletin board above her computer and on it she's tacked up all these letters from the little girl. Like, she still keeps in contact with her even after she found a family to adopt her. I just cried all over again when I saw that."

"I didn't see that—#25 you said?" Maddie literally runs to the backroom to find the comic.

Logan Scott, Maddie's boyfriend and one of the cutest nerds I've ever laid eyes on, comes out of the office. Don't get me wrong, though, he's off-limits. But that doesn't mean I can't admire.

"What are we talking about?" he asks.

"How awesome Finity Girl is," Beth answers.

"Oh yeah, she's a badass. Her power is interesting, if a little confusing. She can stop time, but the power is finite. It will disappear one day. But when?"

"I think they're going to turn that into a major run of issues soon. The Bright Frenzy's title." I tilt my chin up, proud of all the comic-booky lingo I just used.

"You're probably right," he says as Maddie comes back with #25.

She holds it out to me. "Show me the awesome, please? I love hidden Easter eggs in stuff. Like in Pixar movies, how they hide characters from their other movies in each one." I reach for it, but Logan takes it from her first.

"What are we looking for?" He opens the flap of the comic's plastic bag.

She snatches it back from him. "Something you probably didn't notice, either."

He pokes her in her ribs, causing her to jump and let out a little squeal. "Have you forgotten how good I am at exposing what is not obvious to the naked eye?"

"Yeah, yeah, yeah," she says. "But this is Zelda's find. She should have the pleasure."

The back and forth between these two is

adorable, to say the least. Logan is just trying to rile Maddie and she knows exactly what he's doing. I watch as she tips her face up to him and he puts a hand on her waist. They're arguing, but beneath that there's a spark that makes me feel like I'm spying on an intimate moment.

I look away, and jealousy thrums its fingers in my thoughts. Why can't I find a nice guy who likes me for me? I've never had a boyfriend. Never even been kissed. I have plenty of reasons for the state of my life. 1) The pickings are pretty slim in my town. 2) Said pickings have never really shown any interest. 3) The few who did show a slight interest just weren't right. The only time I ever considered someone worthy was Dan. But that was forever ago. When he was only a little taller than me and on the chunky side, I'd thought maybe I'd found someone to hang out with. Then he turned into his present-day persona. I guess I should thank him. Thanks, Dan, for not living up to my imagination. Thanks, Dan, for teaching me a lesson about guys — that they will never measure up to your hopes.

What Maddie and Logan have is a one-in-a-million thing, reserved for very few. I just have to come to terms with that.

Dan will never look at me like Logan looks at Maddie, and that's totally fine. He'll only ever look at me like, well, like he's looking at me right now as he steps through the shop's front door: inconvenienced.

Chapter Six
DAN

The second I step into The Phoenix, Zelda hits me with another one of those stupid glares of hers. Well, I'm not one to keep things bottled up. The question is out before the bell over the door stops ringing. "Why, why, why do you keep looking at me like that?"

She glances at the others around her like she doesn't know full well I'm talking to her. "Who? Me?" She puts a dainty hand to her chest.

I go into a long speech as I walk down the center aisle of the shop. "Cut the innocent act. You're up to something. Every time I see you, you either look at me like you want me to burst into flames or like you know a secret about me. But the thing is, I'm an open book, I have no secrets. So, either you really do want me to burst into flames or you have, like, eye Tourette's. Like you don't have control over them. And if that were the case, then why have I never seen you randomly cross your eyes or blink rapidly?"

Her brows knit together and her lips purse. Then her face relaxes and she freaking crosses her eyes. She turns to everyone else. "I have no idea what this guy is talking about."

They all laugh way too hard for my liking. Logan crosses his eyes, too. "Dude, are you okay? Do you need a glass of water? Maybe a cup of tea?"

"Ha ha, it's all so funny, but I'm serious!" My arms fling out in exasperation. "She's up to something."

Zelda shakes her head and scoffs. "Whatever, Dan."

She's sitting on the counter, so when I try to get in her face, intimidation style, the front of my thighs end up leaning on her knees. I put a hand on either side of hers, which are clutching the counter pretty tightly. I close in so our noses are maybe three or four inches from touching. "You might as well just confess, Zelda. You know I'll figure it out, whatever it is."

She doesn't back down in any way. She just purses those glossy lips again and says, "You are delusional."

The thing is, I pride myself on my ability to be unaffected by the opposite sex. It's a very rare occasion when a girl makes my stomach clench without my permission. So it's a bit of a shock when the tiny hairs on the back of my neck rise at this moment. One side of Zelda's mouth lifts in a defiant grin and her hazel eyes go from plain to nebula-like. My mind is telling me that the attraction I'm feeling can be chalked up to hormones and instinct. The rest of me just wants to see if her lip gloss doesn't only smell like cotton candy but tastes like it, too.

Maddie's voice breaks through the tension. "Oh my God, it's like watching a movie. Don't move, you two, I'm going to make some popcorn."

She's not kidding. She runs into the office and I can hear cabinets opening and closing as she searches for the popcorn. I stand straight and clear my throat. Lowering my voice, I say, "Listen, Z, about the other day in the gym. You know that was an accident, right? I would never hurt you on purpose."

She frowns at me then grabs a comic book. "Whatever."

Well, that's getting frustrating. Here I am trying to sincerely apologize and all I get is a "whatever." I bet her lip gloss tastes nothing like cotton candy.

Logan takes a thick paper bag from a shelf and slaps it on the counter. "I have your pull list right here, dude. It's been sitting here forever though. Why didn't you come in on new comic book day?"

"I've been busy. Practice and games. It's exhausting." I slip my debit card from my wallet.

The sound of the microwave door slamming shut comes from the office as Logan says, "And we haven't seen you at LARP, either. Planning on playing, like, ever again?"

"I just don't have the time. It's painful to talk about, dude. I hate it." I'm not kidding, either. I miss the smell of duct tape and face paint, and the smell of fear that always accompanied my arrival.

"There's a game tonight," Logan says pitifully. And there's another twist to the gut. I haven't hung out with him in ages.

"I can't. There's this stupid fund-raiser thing I have to go to. Taxidermy Todd insists." I shrug.

Logan punches me in the shoulder. "Come on, man. When was the last time you did anything for yourself? You have to have a little fun sometimes. YOLO."

To be honest, I can't remember the last time I went to a movie or played video games until dawn. I'm always on a schedule. Chatting with effyeahFinityGirl is something I have to do on the sly by hiding under the covers with my phone, or by waiting until my parents go to sleep. Would it really be so horrible to miss one little fund-raiser?

I take a moment before I answer, trying to remember the last time I got in big trouble. Finally, I decide I'm due for a little mischief. "Well, you know what they say, 'Only the brave catch the worm.' Fine. I'll be there. But on one condition."

I hear a sigh of frustration from Zelda, who's been reading this whole time, and I cut my eyes at the back of her head. "What?"

"I can't even begin to explain what's wrong with what you just said, because it was such an amalgamation of stupidity."

I open my mouth to deliver a scathing retort, but Logan speaks up, trying to defuse the tension. "What's the condition?"

I decide to let Zelda's comment roll off my back. *Rise above, Garrett.* I turn back to Logan. "You shall never say 'YOLO' again. Like, ever.

Ever, ever, ever."

He laughs. "Done."

"Good. Okay, so if I'm going tonight, then I have to prepare. It's going to be so awesome to dust off Craytor's armor. I'll see you guys later."

A zing of excitement gives my steps a little bounce as I leave the shop. Even Maddie coming out of the office with a fresh bag of popcorn and saying, "Guys, you moved. I said don't move," doesn't upset me. That much.

Zelda's comments and generally pissy attitude do ruffle my feathers, though. I said I was sorry… Or did I? Damn it, maybe I didn't actually say it. But she had to understand I was apologizing, right? I mean, why does she hate me so much? What am I saying? I know why. It's because of me ditching her all that while ago. And because I go out of my way to piss her off sometimes.

I toss my new comics into the passenger seat and slam my door. Then I just sit and marvel at yet another spectacular demonstration of my horrible abilities when it comes to talking to Zelda. Why do I care so much, though? Because I'm a decent human being? That's debatable. Because I like her and if I could choose a girlfriend, she'd be the one? That's about right. Then I remember her very curt "whatever" from a second ago and I frown. Also, why am I even allowing the GF word to pop into my head? I've always been a happily confirmed bachelor. A significant other is just too much hassle. I prefer simple, straightforward relationships like what I have with effyeahFinityGirl.

I nod at my reflection in the rearview mirror, deciding to forget about Zelda Potts and enjoy my time with effyeah. Physical contact is overrated anyway.

Zelda

Why don't things ever work like they're supposed to? I picked up this old bike helmet at the Goodwill and turned it into a great war helm, but the strap isn't staying tight. No wonder someone got rid of it. The stupid thing keeps falling to the side or sliding down to knock my glasses askew as I walk around saying hi to the other players at the game. It throws off the aura I'm trying to create. I'm a battle-hardened, dwarf shield maiden named Bronla, damn it, not a goofy noob.

I can't handle it anymore so I take off my

helm and set it on one of the fold-out tables the gamemasters have set up in the backyard. It's a really nice night out, perfect for a little nerdery. It's a rare Louisiana winter evening, which just means it's not raining. And they've put speakers outside so they can play epic fantasy movie soundtracks to set the mood, which it's definitely doing.

"Nice work on the helmet, dude," someone says from behind me.

I turn to graciously accept the compliment. "Of course it is. I made it, after all," I say then realize who I'm talking to.

I should have known Dan would be making his annoying appearance at some point. I didn't really believe him at the comic shop when he said he was coming, nor did I believe him about the basketball incident, but effyeahFinityGirl got a message earlier from him saying he was going to the LARP game but that didn't mean he couldn't chat. And she, I, replied with, "Oh, LARPing? That sounds like so much fun! I've never been. Give me a play by play if you think of it!"

It was a spur of the moment request. I figured I need to prove that his new station in life has changed his view on those of us who don't have the world at their feet. So, if he started slamming his fellow gamers, a group in which he used to proudly count himself, there it would be: my proof. Now I'm torn as to whether or not I want him to keep FinityGirl updated. What if he tells her stuff that me/Bronla wouldn't know in character? What if I accidentally use that information later and unintentionally cheat? I'm not exactly batting a thousand when it comes to moral fiber at the moment, and I'd rather not make it worse.

He lets out a big, fake *Ha!* "Well, aren't we modest. It is pretty boss, though. Is it comfortable? That's the true mark of great craftsmanship."

I'm too shocked to stop him before he puts the helmet on his head. How dare he?! But of course, it fits him perfectly. Wearing the helmet and the armor he bought on eBay, which was advertised as "an early test chest plate from the costume department for the *Lord of the Rings: The Two Towers*," he could easily be mistaken for a young warrior of Rohan.

"How do I look?" He strikes a hero pose with his fists on his hips and his face turned to the side so his profile looks regal and strong. He's positioned perfectly in front of the back porch light so it creates a golden halo around his head and shoulders.

When I start to wonder if I was wrong when I told Beth, "The Gondor men are way hotter than the guys from Rohan," I snatch my helmet off his head. I do not like my nerd opinions to be called into question, especially not because of Dan Garrett.

"You look like an imposter. A tall, impostering imposter." I know my tone sounds bitter, but I don't care.

"Excuse me? You're lucky my rank in the king's guard exceeds yours by so much, or I might give your insult notice."

I roll my eyes. "Oh please, get off your high horse. You haven't been here in forever. I'd be willing to bet I'm actually the higher rank now."

He holds his hand out. "Prove it. Gimme your character sheet."

It's my turn to fake laugh at him. "Ha! No." There's no way I'm going to let him see all my powers or Bronla's secret origin story. Keeping your character's skeletons in the closet and surprising people with powers is all part of the game.

His eyes narrow at me and I narrow mine right back at him. The tension, you could cut it with a lightsaber.

From across the backyard, Maddie's voice sounds all high-pitched and giddy. "Oh my God, it's happening again. They're doing the thing, come on!"

I step back from Dan and watch Maddie tug Logan behind her. They're playing as their elves, Laowyn and Graffin, tonight, and they look awesome. Maddie's sparkly leggings and shimmering face powder have made me contemplate playing an elf or fairy on many occasions, but I always remember how great it feels to defeat a foe using straight-up strength instead of magic. Maybe I'll channel my need for girly glitter into Bronla's weapon, which I've yet to make, because not only is glitter awesome, but it can also be a weapon itself. A spec of glitter can turn into a tiny razor blade if it gets in your eye.

Maddie and Logan make it over to us, and her face falls in disappointment. "Why don't you guys ever listen to me? Do the thing again. And go."

"Cut it out, cheerleader. The game is starting." Dan nods to the middle of the yard where Tommy, one of the gamemasters, stands beneath a large magnolia tree, holding his arms up for silence.

As Tommy goes over the rules of the game, which I've heard a million times, I go over my goals for tonight in my head. I'll need to do some major feats in order to get enough experience points so I can up my rage level. And I'd like to make friends with some of the fairies who always have the best potions. It'd also be nice to develop some sort of alliance with the vampires, because they know everyone's secrets.

Tommy's last announcement breaks into my thoughts. "I'll need volunteers for a mission tonight. Know that the mission is treacherous but the rewards are high."

Perfect, that's just what I need for the XP.

"Who will lend us their bravery?" Tommy asks, channeling Gandalf the Grey.

I throw my fist in the air and shout, "You have my shield and ax!" But my words have an echo. I look to my left and see Dan scowling at me, his fist in the air as well.

If I wasn't concerned with getting a butt-ton of XP this game, I'd drop out of the mission this very instant. But I will not be cheated out of my next level-up by Dan-freaking-Garrett.

Tommy motions for the volunteers to follow him into the kitchen, or "the war room" as he calls it.

"Have fun, you two. Don't kill each other," Logan calls out as we walk behind Tommy.

In the "war room," it's me, Dan, a fairy I've only seen a couple of times at the game, and a vampire who's been playing for years. So, it looks like I'll be sticking by the vampire while trying to protect the fairy who can't possibly be advanced enough for this mission. And all the while, I'll be trying to *not* punch Dan in the throat. Just another fun night of pretend life.

While Tommy runs to his room to get reference books and stuff he'll need to prepare for this, Dan whips out his phone. A few seconds later, my phone vibrates in my pocket. Of course Dan couldn't wait to bitch about something to effyeahFinityGirl.

I excuse myself to go to the bathroom, but when I'm there, I almost resist the temptation to check Dan's message. Curiosity wins out fast, though. I've just got to hope he's not about to reveal something super juicy about the vampire in our group or anything. I like to think I'm good at this game but when it comes to separating things I know out of character from things I know in character, it gets tricky.

Dantheman: Remember that girl I was talking about? The one I blew it with and now she hates me?

Why does he want to talk about this now? Whatever, I guess I shouldn't look a gift horse in the mouth.

Me: Vaguely, why?

Dantheman: She's here and she still hates me and now we have to go on a mission together.

Chapter Seven
DAN

Jommy comes back with all the stuff he needs to give us our mission. Jason, a.k.a. Gregor the vampire, has been playing this game since before I ever joined, so it's going to be tough to outdo him.

The fairy's name is Julie, and she's very excited to be here. "I'll probably die but that's okay because just the experience is great, ya know? And I love your armor! Where did you get it? I went to a Renn fair once and there were some awesome knight guys on horses and stuff. Their armor was pretty cool, too. Have you ever been to a Renn fair? You should try it." And on and on she goes.

My phone dings, so I have a reason to step away from Excited Julie.

effyeahFinityGirl: What are you going to do?

That's the question of the night, isn't it? When I got here, I reminded myself that even if I saw Zelda, I wouldn't engage. I would ignore. I would not care. Then I saw her and my normally cold, black heart rebelled. Apparently it doesn't matter how many times I tell myself that I can just forget about her, because the second she comes into view I wish she didn't straight-up hate me. And that's exactly the situation with her. I don't care what Logan or Maddie say. I talked to them when I got here and saw Zelda bouncing from person to person in the backyard. The whole time she fidgeted with that helmet.

"She really needs to just take that thing off before it causes her to fall or something," I'd said. It was just an observation, but Maddie blew it way out of proportion.

"Aw, you're protective of her. You two are adorable. Go talk to her." She shoved me surprisingly hard in the back.

"I am not protective of her. I'm a conscientious observer. Don't you know how clumsy she is? She basically supports the Band-Aid and ice pack industry," I said, dodging Maddie's attempts to get me to move in Zelda's direction.

In the end, Maddie pulled out a play that was hitting below the belt to get me to go talk to the girl. "So, you're afraid of her then?" She tilted her stupid head and crossed her stupid arms.

Logan literally gasped.

The story of how Maddie figured out that one simple statement could get me to do anything is a long and complicated one involving a vintage Playstation 2 game and Maddie's inhuman ability to kick everyone's ass in it. We all have those irrational things that can really get under our skin, no matter how thick said skin is. Someone insinuating that I'm afraid is my thing.

So, I tried to make conversation with Zelda. And it ended horribly, as all our interactions seem to. I'm not surprised at the way things went, just disappointed. Which is why I messaged FinityGirl. An outside opinion would be welcome at the moment.

Me: What am I going to do? I have no idea.

Zelda finally comes back from the bathroom, and something is a little off, but I can't get a read on her. She won't turn her face fully in my direction. Then Tommy jumps into the mission at hand and it's time to put everything else aside. I'll put Zelda's loathing, along with Maddie's ability to mind control my behavior, over on this shelf marked "deal with later."

We follow Tommy to the stairs that lead up as he speaks. "A pecan farm a little outside the city limits has been inexplicably turned into a labyrinth." His British accent has gotten a million times better since the last time I was here, I'll give him that. "The council is concerned, even though no one has been stupid enough to enter the maze and get themselves killed. Yet." He crosses his fingers, signifying that he is talking "out of character" as he says the next bit. "You've probably all seen this place before. It's a large field filled with really old pecan trees. They are planted in rows with the grass trimmed beneath them. Sometimes the owners let the cattle run free in the field, their hulking bodies snorting beneath the gigantic barken trunks, their breath visible in the dewy morning air as the sun rises over—"

I hold my crossed fingers up and interrupt him. "Dude, can we get on with it? Your third year creative writing class is doing wonders for your descriptive prose, but I'm ready to smash some skulls."

It takes all I have to not squeak in shock when Zelda actually seconds my statement with a fervent nod.

Tommy sighs and flips past one, two, three of the notecards he was reading from. The dude must really be digging those writing classes.

"Okay, here we go. Those fields you knew so well have now changed. A heavy fog cradles the area and the trees are surrounded by a very tall stone wall." He removes the tape and sign saying OFF-LIMITS from the posts at the bottom of the stairs. "This is the only entrance. What do you do?"

I speak up, knowing how this stuff works. "I walk the perimeter, looking for weak spots."

Gregor the vamp flips his long cape, which I'm pretty sure was made out of curtains, over his shoulder. "I fly up and test the space above the wall using the 'Danger, out thee' power."

"I go through the entrance," Excited Julie says, but before I can tell her, *no no no, don't do that*, Zelda puts a hand on her shoulder.

"Let's wait here for them. We should explore all the possibilities and be cautious. I use my abilities of tracking in combination with heightened senses to investigate the entrance." Zelda pulls out her character sheet from the inside of her helmet and I could kick myself. It was sitting on my head at the same time as I asked her for it.

She shows it to Tommy and his eyes widen a little. "Wow, I didn't realize you'd pumped this up so much. How long do you want to keep these abilities active?"

"Until I'm down to one power point." She grins. That little minx is a smart cookie. She'll be able to know about anything and everything around us while we go through the maze. She'll catch the scent of an enemy, hear the twang of a trip wire or the click of a hidden door opening. To be honest, she just positioned herself as the most important asset to the group.

Tommy nods and flips through his notes. "All right, Craytor, you find no weak spots. Gregor, you take two points damage when you test the space above the wall. Do you want to keep trying?"

Gregor shakes his head then pulls out a small black velvet bag. He removes two deep red marbles from it and puts them in his pants pocket. Silly vamps, they always have to make a scene even over losing two tiny life points.

"Bronla, you find an inscription next to the entrance of the labyrinth. It says, 'Heed my warning, forbidden is the center. The mist is forming and the night is storming. It would be folly to enter.' Who's doing what now?"

After much bickering, mostly from Gregor, who keeps trying to use all his super special powers for no reason, we all finally decide to just enter the maze. Tommy leads us up the stairs and we fight nasty creatures along the way. Everyone holds their own, except for poor Excited Julie. By the time we make it to the upper floor, she's down to her last health potion.

Every room upstairs represents some scary portion of the maze, and Craytor dominates no matter what we go up against. Then Zelda does something suspicious. She takes Tommy aside and they whisper for a bit before coming back to the rest of the group.

There is no way I'm going to let that slide, of course. "What was that all about?"

She adjusts her helmet for the millionth time. "None of your business, imposter."

And there she goes with the automatic hostility again. "Well, *sorry*. Why do you keep calling me an imposter?"

She lets out a frustrated sigh and follows the others to the next room/cave of death.

I literally throw my hands up. I'm so done with this game of hers. I don't deserve this. My cold, black heart returns to its old self.

Zelda

Does he really need it explained to him? Do I have to be the one to tell him that he lost his nerd cred a long time ago?

Dan comes into the room and leans against the wall, arms crossed. Whatever, I can't be distracted right now. The big baddie battle is next, and it's going to be Bronla's time to shine.

I know that the final battle is about to happen because there's only one room left on the second floor. The house hangout room, as the guys who live here call it, has been decorated as sinisterly as possible. Apparently, college guys think ominous equals a ton of candles, most of them scented and none of them the same scent, and red twinkle lights. It does the job.

Tommy tugs on his earlobe, which is our

agreed-upon signal, so I casually go over to talk to him. Earlier I'd asked him to tell me in private if my enhanced senses caught anything, especially a trap of any sort. The secret signal was his idea, though. He does have a flare for the dramatic.

He whispers, "Bronla's senses prickle and she notices a vicious-looking vine covering the wall. Your level of monster knowledge is high enough that you know it's Thief's Menace."

"Which wall?" I ask.

"To the left of the entrance."

"You mean the one Craytor is leaning against right now?" I ask, not even trying to hide my excitement.

Tommy nods. "Yes ma'am. You should probably warn him. Do you?"

How shitty would it be of me if I didn't warn him? One of the big things you learn when you start playing this game is that unless your fingers are crossed, your character is doing and saying whatever you're doing or saying. Dan should know not to touch anything unless he's completely sure it's not dangerous. Or maybe he's so confident in his character's abilities that he thinks he can take on anything and he doesn't have to be careful. Yes, that's the vibe I'll go with. He needs a reminder. It'll make him a better player in the end if I don't warn him.

I shake my head in the negative.

Tommy must take pity on Dan/Craytor because he asks, "Dude, are you leaning against the wall like that in character?"

Dan shrugs. "Yeah, sure, whatever." He pulls out his phone and taps away at it.

I'm feeling really good about my decision to not warn Craytor about the dwarf-killing plant he's currently snuggling against. Then my phone vibrates.

While Tommy goes over to supervise the fight that's about to happen between Craytor and the Thief's Menace, I check my messages.

I admit, it was a bit of a shock when I realized Dan had been talking about me—that I was the girl he thinks he blew it with. Okay, fine, "a bit of a shock" is an understatement. It was like watching a movie and everything is calm, the characters are having a boring conversation, then BAM: explosions, death, destruction, nothing will ever be the same again!

It took me a while to get my breathing under control, and my brain turned to mush for a good five minutes. Hell, realizing that he even thinks about me at all was... Disturbing? Unbelievable?

A revelation? Basically, I have no idea how to feel about this. And for a while at the beginning of the mission, I thought that maybe I could ease up on him. Then he started being really cocky, killing all the enemies with one swing, pretending he was our leader, and I lost all sympathy for him. And this new message doesn't do him any favors.

> **Dantheman:** That's it. I'm so done with this girl. I've tried being nice. I've tried making conversation and all she does is call me an imposter and I don't get it.

Being nice? Sure, he complimented my helmet, but that was canceled out by an immediate jerk maneuver. And if he thinks "making conversation" equals pushing past me to take on a fight I obviously had under control, while saying, "Let me handle this, sweetheart," he's horribly mistaken.

I decide to not respond to his message because I don't trust myself to not reveal my identity in some way. I mean, if I were to say what I want to say, which is, "Are you sure you're *not* being a raging toolbag to this girl?" he might get suspicious.

"Okay," Tommy says as he positions himself in the middle of the room, "while you all were looking around the room, Craytor was captured by a Thief's Menace. He fought it and won, but he was poisoned by the Menace's thorns and is at a severe disadvantage."

I glance over my shoulder at Dan. Slowly, he holds up his crossed fingers and mouths the words, "I hate you."

I smile and cross my fingers, too. "Sorry. Just playing the game, dude."

He rolls his eyes and I turn my attention back to Tommy.

"You've entered the Sphinx's lair. The creature's snores echo through—"

Gregor interrupts Tommy with crossed fingers. "Don't you mean a minotaur? There was never a sphinx in a labyrinth."

Tommy goes quiet and stares at the ceiling for a second. "Well, there's a sphinx in this one, okay? Can we just get through this?"

Gregor shrugs.

The final battle involves a riddle, but no one knows the answer, so we just attack. Dan/Craytor is knocked unconscious pretty quickly. Gregor tries to use all his special powers, but his dice rolls are horrible so he doesn't succeed in much. He runs out of magic juice fast. My rolls, on the other hand, are so on point, it's ridiculous. I'm cracking this thing's skull left and right. It's critical hit after critical hit, and it's glorious. I'm even distracting the thing sufficiently enough that it's not paying attention to Julie, whose little zaps of fairy magic aren't doing much damage at all.

Even Dan's stupid peanut gallery comments don't affect me…that much. Most of it is him doing that thing where he knows that I know what I should do next, so he says it right before I do it to make it seem like he's coaching me. So annoying.

"Drink a health potion!" he yells.

"I know."

"Aim for the gem thing on his chest!"

"I know."

"Turn on your 'Resist confound' prowess! I bet he has some sort of confusion power!"

"I…know."

Okay, that last one was sort of helpful, but I'm not going to actually tell him that.

Like these things usually do, it takes a good thirty to forty-five minutes to get the sphinx down to his last bit of life. Just as I'm about to finish it off, Julie decides to do something rash.

She steps between Tommy and me. "I've got this, friend." She's totally not trying to steal the glory/XP points. She's just trying to participate, ya know.

"I fly at its face and unleash a swarm of fireflies with my last few magic points."

I admire her bravery but this is a bad, bad idea. Her swarm just won't do enough damage to kill the sphinx, and this move will put her in its eyesight. It'll turn its attention to her and she'll die a horrible, confounded death. The sphinx will swat her to the ground with its cat paw and squash her like a mosquito.

I have a chance to save her, though. Every power takes a certain amount of game seconds to occur. I know the swarm takes ten seconds. My most powerful spell takes seven. My health is already so low that I can only take one maybe two more hits from this thing and this spell will totally deplete my magic points.

It's perfectly in line with my character's levels of loyalty, bravery, and goodness that she would potentially sacrifice herself instead of letting this noob fairy die.

"Wait! My spell will precede hers!" I yell like I'm really inside an echoing chamber with all kinds of explosions and battle sounds going on around me. "I cast 'Straight and True' on my hammer and throw it at the gem."

I hear a gasp that would normally be inaudible,

but it's as loud as a gunshot because Dan's mouth is directly next to my ear. I jump and turn to him. His eyes are glued to my character sheet, which I've been holding this whole time.

I hug it to my chest and shove him away. "Stop peeking!"

"Are you sure you want to do that? You'll be dead in, like, one turn if you don't roll above a"—he looks at the ceiling and does some mental calculation—"a thirteen! That's not lucky at all. That's the definition of unlucky, Z."

I don't care about the note of concern in his voice. I still roll my eyes at him.

I turn to Tommy and nod. "I cast it."

These types of moments don't happen often during gameplay. This is potentially life or death. Everyone watches, breath held, as I toss a twenty-sided die onto the coffee table. The die tumbles, clicking its way across the glossy wood, then stops. We all lean in, my helmet bumping against Dan's head, to see the outcome.

It's a ten. Bronla, the character I've been working on for months and months, is so dead.

Chapter Eight
DAN

Wow. Just wow. That was the most heartbreaking thing I believe I've ever seen. I felt so bad for Zelda earlier at the game that I didn't even say, "I told you so." When that ten fell, silence flattened the room. It took a good minute or two before Tommy spoke.

"Okay, so let's do the math." He tapped away at his calculator, all the while mumbling, "maybe, just maybe," but in the end that ten, even with some generous multipliers from Gregor's vamp, didn't get the job done. The sphinx knocked Zelda beyond incapacitation and into death the next round. But

Zelda's move did distract it long enough for the fairy to ping off the sphinx's last few health points.

I thought about trying to comfort Zelda, but for the first time in months I didn't want to see her turn to me with vibrant fury in her eyes. I wanted her to be happy, to feel better, and I knew nothing I could say would accomplish that, no matter how sincere I sounded.

After experience points were solemnly dealt out, Julie grabbed an in-shock Zelda by the shoulders and pulled her into a hug. "I'll never forget what you did. Bronla will live on in my character's mind for eternity."

"Thanks," Zelda said in a timid voice.

I recognized that voice. I heard it when we watched *The Lion King* together in ninth grade during the scene when Simba's dad dies. I heard it when Zelda called to tell me about her dad forgetting to send her a birthday card. I knew what that tone of voice meant, and the sound of it made my cold, black heart turn to a pile of mush.

The others left the room then, but Zelda didn't seem to want to move. She just kind of stood there staring at that stupid ten, still hugging her character sheet to her chest.

I couldn't say anything, and I wouldn't leave her

there, so instead I put my hand on her upper back as lightly as I could. I steered her down the stairs, through the house, and into the backyard. People stared and whispered as we passed because news travels during a LARP game just like it does in a small town: quick and super exaggerated.

I found Maddie and Logan sitting together on the porch swing. "Maddie?" I called.

She looked up, a frown immediately taking over her face. "Oh, Zelda, I'm so sorry. Come with me." They disappeared back into the house and I dropped onto the seat with Logan.

"Dude…" he said.

I rubbed the back of my neck to hopefully relieve some tension. "I know."

"That sucks."

"I know."

He leaned forward, putting his elbows on his knees. "I mean, people outside of this might think it's silly to get all worked up over a fictional character, but when you create something, put time and effort into making it better, deal with it for months, then just like that"—he emphasized his words with a snap of his fingers—"it's gone? That can really take a toll on a person."

"So true."

I didn't see Zelda for the rest of the night, which is why I'm now staring at my phone debating on whether or not to give her a call to confer my condolences. There's a quick one-knock on my door and Dad steps into my room. "How did everything go at the fund-raiser?"

I've been dreading this. I flipping hate lying to my parents. "Great. Nothing crazy to report."

"Are you sure? Nothing at all?" What is he doing? He's acting weird. He shuffles around my room a little, not making eye contact. My dad is a straight-forward, business-minded man. The kind of guy who believes in a firm handshake and Johnny Cash. So when he fiddles with the Lego Millennium Falcon that hangs from my ceiling, I know something is up. Or am I projecting my guilt onto the situation and over thinking?

I stick with my lie. "Nope. Nothing."

He jerks his worn cap off his head and slaps it hard against his thigh. I've made an epic mistake. "Damn it, Daniel. You're lying to me. I called your coach to make sure the team got the money they needed for the new equipment, and he told me you weren't there."

No point in denying it now. "Okay, I didn't go. It's not that big of a deal, though. Missing one fund-raiser isn't so bad."

His face goes red at that. "Not a big deal? You made a commitment. This isn't a game, Daniel."

And here's the point where my smart-ass mouth speaks without my go-ahead. "Actually, it is. There's this ball, and we throw it through a hoop, and there's a scoreboard. That's exactly what this is. A game."

Anger flashes in his eyes, and he crushes his cap in his hand. "Where were you? You must've been somewhere more important, right? To miss something that pertains to your athletic career, to your potential college career? And don't tell me you were rescuing some old lady's cat from a tree or helping a blind man cross the street, because I'm tired of your smart mouth."

I could make something up. I probably should. But I'm so tired. I'm tired of pretending that I'm the perfect son, that basketball and school are the only things of any importance to me. "I was at a LARP game, okay?"

Dad rolls his eyes. His voice has now officially hit the "seriously pissed off" stage. "How many times have I told you? That crap is pointless. It does nothing but distract you from the important stuff. It's a waste of time. Do you want to finish high school as just another mediocre student? Or do you want to be one of the best? I stood by when you were younger and let you play dress up, but that time is over now. No more, Daniel. You have so much potential. I don't want all our work to be for nothing. Do you realize how many people I've had to talk to in order to get the talent scout from LSU to even *consider* watching one of your games? You can't do this kind of stuff."

He might've hit the "seriously pissed off" stage, but I've just hit the "I don't care" stage. "Yes, sir. Whatever you say, sir. I'm sorry, sir."

He tilts his chin up and I can see the gears turning in his head. He's wondering if I'm being sarcastic, or placating him. "Right, then. No more games. No more ditching the *important* stuff. If something like this happens again, I'll have to take away some privileges. I'll start with your car."

I don't say anything about that because I didn't want that monstrosity in the first place. I would have been content with something a little less Kanye.

"The next thing to go will be your laptop and phone."

This gets my undivided attention. I subtract the attitude from my voice. "Yes sir. No more distractions. I promise."

He nods, satisfied that I'm definitely not being sarcastic this time. "Good. Now get some sleep."

When he leaves, I punch one of my pillows a good ten times. Why couldn't I have had one of those hippy dads? The kind who's willing to talk things out instead of just dictating? There's no way I can lose my internet connection right now. Putting on a face at school, pretending I like those people because confrontation is not my jam, is exhausting. Losing my connection would mean losing effyeahFinityGirl, which would be like losing the only person in the world who understands me.

Zelda

The loss of Bronla felt practically like a death in the family, and the way Dan was kind of nice to me is throwing my carefully crafted plan out of whack. I should be much further along with my social experiment. By this point, considering the amount of chats we've had, I should at least have some kind of proof that popularity, being liked by everyone for innocuous reasons, changes a person for the worse. But all I have written is a bunch of stuff about how he *used* to be and all the things he's done up to this point.

Maybe he's just pretending to be the kind of guy FinityGirl would like. Maybe I should've been a guy when I started this whole thing, and then he would've been more genuine. Because there's no way this is how he actually is, right?

When Dan's an hour late to our agreed-upon chat time, I try to muster up some of the confidence I felt when I started chatting with him as FinityGirl, but that's all shot to hell with his first comment.

Dantheman: Sorry I'm late. Just had a big fight with my dad. I hate fighting with him.

Oh no. If there's one person in this world that means more to Dan than himself, it's his dad. They've always had the kind of father/son relationship you only see on fifties sitcoms. Sure, they fight like any parent and child do, but nothing that's ever really serious. At least, that's the way it used to be. I remember being jealous of them, how Taxidermy Todd would slap Dan on the back with a big grin when he would correct his grammar. Mr. Garrett was always nice to me, too. He made sure Dan and I watched the Star Wars movies in what he thought was the correct order. I'd never really seen a father be, well…a real father.

Me: I'm sorry. Wanna talk about it?

Dantheman: It's the same old story. The pressure he's putting on me about basketball and college is driving me bat-balls crazy. It's hard to have any fun at all. There's so much pressure to be the best, to succeed.

Me: Have you explained that to him? That you feel stressed.

Dantheman: Feelings? What are these things you speak of? There's no crying in basketball! What I mean to say is my dad isn't exactly a "feelings" type of guy.

I can't argue with him on that. His dad is not a softy by any means.

Me: Well, from what I can tell, you guys are close. Maybe you're not giving him enough credit? Maybe he would understand. Honesty is the best policy, after all.

I cringe at my last sentence. The hypocrisy is strong with this one.

Dantheman: I guess you're right. I do

want to be honest with him because it might improve my quality of life, and we'd understand each other better. Then again, I could just bear with it until college, when I'll be free.

Me: You might think you'll be free, but I'm willing to bet that your dad will just continue to put pressure on you about the next big thing. That kind of stuff can cause serious emotional damage to a person.

He's quiet for a long time. This conversation got way more intense than I was expecting. Time to lighten the mood.

Me: Or you could just play a game that's a great stress reliever. I hear *Shoot Your Face Anywhere* on the new handheld is good for that.

Dantheman: I freaking love that game! Do you have it? We could play!

Ha! Do I have the newest handheld gaming device? I'm lucky if my first year Nintendo DS runs for ten minutes.

Me: Unfortunately, no. I've been saving up for one, though.

Mental note to self: start saving up. And not because I could potentially kick Dan's butt in this game, because there's no "potentially" about it, but because everyone needs goals in life.

Dantheman: Damn. Hey, thanks for listening to me whine about my stupid problems.

"Awww," I say. Out loud. To no one at all. What the hell is wrong with me? And why am I constantly asking that question lately? I know why, though. It's him. It's all his fault. When he's standing in front of me, it's easy to despise him. But here, in our little corner of the internet, I feel like I'm just a girl talking to just a guy. It's infuriating.

Me: It's no biggie. :)

There's a pause in conversation where I don't know what else to say. I have this weird feeling like this is a turning point, but it can't be that big of a thing, right? That I was there for him? I can't be the only person he feels comfortable talking to about personal things.

Dantheman: Can I be totally honest real quick? And if what I'm about to say makes you uncomfortable, just block it out for the rest of time, okay?

How ominous can you get, Dan?

Me: Sure, go ahead.

Dantheman: I think you're awesome and amazing. Probably one of the coolest girls I've ever met. One of the coolest people I've ever met, in fact. I don't have many friends. Not real ones, anyway.

Nope nope nope. This isn't what I want to hear! I have to stop him before he endears himself to me anymore.

Me: Thanks, dude! I gotta go, though. Talk to you later, okay?

I don't even wait for his response. I log off and sit back. What have I gotten myself into?

Chapter Nine
DAN

I've heard the stories about people finding their soul mates on the internet, but those were mostly from online dating site commercials. And I never actually believed them. But I'm not one to deny something that's plain in front of my face.

The conversations with this girl are fantastic. She's extremely smart. Dare I say, maybe smarter than me? *Maybe.* I double-check our chats on my phone when I get to first period to assure myself that I'm not making up the awesomeness that has happened.

Of course, I've been charming without being cheesy. She's been cute in all the ways I like a girl to be cute. She only uses one emoticon and that's the one for flipping a table in anger, which is fantastic. The occasional smiley face I can forgive. Plus, it was me who brought up the idea that we continue chatting, not her, which is a good sign that she is in fact a girl around my age and not a thirty-year-old dude hanging out in his basement.

Would it be weird to message her now? It hasn't even been eight hours since we chatted last. I wanted to confess more last night. I wanted to say that she's been a lighthouse during a storm on the sea. She's been a much-needed confidante. Should I say all those things now? In the light of day, it sounds so sappy, but I mean every bit of it. Or should I see her quick disappearance as fate? As a sort of time to check myself?

Class starts, taking the decision out of my hands, but that doesn't mean I can't spend the next hour or so totally not paying attention to Mr. Boggin's lecture on *Of Mice and Men*, and instead figuring out the most intriguing yet unique thing to say to effyeahFinityGirl.

By the time first period is over, I have almost perfected it, but it still needs some polishing. I am debating between, "How is your day going?" or "Today's public schooling system boggles my mind. Why are we studying tomes that are so ancient? Does *Of Mice and Men* really teach us something that we can't learn by reading something more contemporary and relatable? In fact, I'm almost positive I read a *Star Trek* novel that tackled some of the same ideas as *OMaM*."

As I'm walking to my locker, I get this overwhelming feeling that it would be freaking awesome to say these things to this girl in real life. We've only been talking for a couple of weeks. Would it be too soon to ask to meet? Hell if I know. I'm not good at these types of interactions. Females are confusing creatures. Plus, I have no idea where she lives. She could be in Tokyo for all I know.

Another shocking thought pops into my head. *I wish I could talk to Maddie about this.* Frightening, isn't it? That I would need or want the cheerleader's help not just once but twice in such a short period of time. What is happening to me? But it would be nice to have her opinion. Then again, she'd probably make fun of me or start pushing me to talk about Zelda. But who else will be knowledgeable about this kind of stuff?

I close my locker and pull out my phone, quickly typing in a text to Maddie. Then I slam into someone, both of us knocking each other back a few steps.

"Whoa, sorry about—" Zelda realizes who she's talking to and loses the apologetic tone faster than Quicksilver after drinking a Red Bull. "Aren't you watching where you're going? Oh, I guess not." She nods at the phone in my hand.

"First off, I'm sorry. Second off, why didn't you dodge me if you were paying attention?" I lean down and pick up her phone, which she dropped. I shake my head and *tsk tsk tsk* at her. "Hypocritical much?"

She rolls her eyes and stomps her foot. I'd call the action cute if I didn't know this girl wouldn't hesitate to take out her frustration on a part of my body that is very near and dear to me. A part of my body that holds the future of the Garrett line. The part that could potentially, wait, who am I kidding, that *will probably* produce the first All Powerful, All Knowing Ambassador of the Earth...That would be my genitals, to be clear.

"Whatever. Give it back." She holds her hand out, and I notice her fingernails are painted the most sparkly, bluey, greeny, aqua, turquoise color

I've ever seen.

"Wow!" I shield my eyes like I'm a vampire stepping into the sun's rays. "That's a... Yeah, I can't find a complimentary way of saying eye-pain-making color."

She looks at her nails. "It's called Medusa's Hair Appointment and it's awesome. Now, give me my phone."

I go to put the phone in her hand then jerk it back. "Wait, since I have your rapt attention... You don't still think I hit you with that basketball on purpose the other day, do you?"

Her gaze doesn't shift from her phone. "Just stop it." She flips her long, thick braid over her shoulder and her jaw clenches like there are a lot of words in her mouth trying to fight their way out.

I let out a pissed-off huff. "Fine. I'm sorry, for what it's worth, which is probably nothing to you, but there you go. My new shoes tripped me up, it was an accident, I hate that it happened, and I'm sorry."

She frowns a little, then shakes whatever thoughts she was having from her head. "Don't care. I'm over it. Just give me my phone so I can leave your tedious presence."

Gotta love it when a girl sounds like she just stepped out of a period movie about old chaps, matrons, and wealthy estates. An idea hits me then. She's a girl and I'm assuming she knows how girls think. Maybe she can help me figure out what to do about effyeah. "Zelda, you're a smart person of the female variety. Can I ask you something?"

Her brows knit together and cheeks redden. "Oh my God, Dan Garrett, shut up and give me my phone!"

She tries to snatch the phone from my hand, but I'm faster. And taller. I hold it at my full reach above my head. She jumps for it, using my shoulder to help hoist her up, and I have to smile. This feels better, like I'm making progress with her. It's the first time she's touched me since that forearm to the gut in the gym. And not only is this physical contact a lot less painful than the last, it comes with what I can only describe as pretty-girl-smell.

I laugh at her second attempt to reach the phone. "Just hear me out. I—" That's when the warning bell for class sounds from the PA system, and we both look around to see we're practically the only two left in the hallway. "Crap, I have to get to class. I'll see you at lunch?"

Zelda

I'm not just going to kill him. I'm going to decimate him. I'm going to eviscerate him in fiction. If there isn't already a category on my fanfic site called "Dan Garrett, how I hate thee, let me count the ways," then I'm going to make one.

I can't catch up to him in the hallway. Damn his long legs and actual exercise regimen. The door to his class closes behind him just as I reach it. I fling it open and all eyes turn to me. Miss Greer's eyes included.

"Can I help you, Miss Potts?" she asks.

I open my mouth. Close it. Then open it again. "Sorry. Wrong room."

Dan glances at the screen of my phone as he sits in his desk on the other side of the room. The door clicks closed in my face.

I'm doomed.

I don't even make an attempt to rush to class. It's drama and the only reason I took it is because the teacher is really laid back. A group of four people are huddled outside the class, practicing lines for the upcoming production of *Taming of the Shrew* when I trudge up, dragging my backpack behind me. The only notice they give me consists of scoffs and eye rolls when I interrupt their rehearsal by shoving through the center of them.

Mr. Drew, the teacher, is having an animated discussion with one of the resident stoner musician guys, so I collapse in a desk next to Beth.

She doesn't say anything for a long time. She just stares at me. I guess I deserve to be stared at, considering I probably look like my goldfish just died.

Finally, she asks, "Soooo, how did it go last night? What are you on now? Date number ten? Eleven?" She props her chin on her palm and her big, almost anime-like eyes try to read my thoughts. It shouldn't be too hard for her to do. I'm not trying to hide the fact that life is about to get really hard.

And the "date"? It was…kind of awesome. Granted, I haven't gotten any super juicy tidbits out of Dan, but surprisingly, I've had fun. So much fun that on most nights we don't stop talking until two in the morning. Not to mention that last night I actually felt, gasp, sympathy for him.

All day, I'd been reliving our "dates." I even checked back over the chats on my phone because I was sure I've said or done *something* that would reveal who I really am or something that was incredibly loser-ish. But I couldn't find anything. After that, I wanted to message him, but I couldn't get it right. I didn't know if I should say, "Did I keep you up too late?" or "American history is so messed up. Are we being taught the reality of what happened or the holiday/commercialized version? I find it hard to believe Native Americans were cool with sitting down to break bread with those interlopers."

Then he had to make an appearance and shatter all my happy feels. There he was, the exact guy I was about to message. Dan Garrett with his stupid, hilarious T-shirt featuring two AT-ATs humping and his mussed but dying-for-fingers-to-run-through-it dusty brown hair.

And now I hate myself even more for just thinking that.

"So?" Beth asks again.

What do I tell her? Do I tell her that I'm so severely screwed that I'm considering a full-on witness protection lifestyle? Because that's pretty much my only course of action at this point.

Dan has what amounts to my entire life in the palm of his hand. He'll see our chats. He'll see the texts I sent to Beth about him and my plan. And what did I think was going to happen? Did I really think I could pull off some only-works-in-movies shit?

"Do you think it could be possible that Dan didn't mean to hit me with that basketball?" The question flies out of my mouth, and I don't remember thinking about asking it.

She scowls, looking me up and down. "Are you okay? I mean, I can tell you're not. Was he that big of a jerk last night?"

I shake my head and pick at my nail polish. It's not chipping yet, but it's inevitable, so why not just go ahead and get it over with? "No, I'm fine. He was fine. I just… I don't know."

She puts a worried hand on my shoulder. "What happened, Z? Tell me."

I let my forehead hit the surface of my desk. It hurts. "He has my phone."

A bit of time passes where she doesn't say anything. I just wait for the moment of realization to explode from her.

"Holy shit! Don't tell me your chat is on there!"

There it is.

I nod my head, which probably just looks like I'm rubbing it up and down on my desk.

"Please tell me it's password protected or something."

I shake my head, again seemingly nuzzling my desk.

"Zelda, do you have your homework?" Mr. Drew asks from above me.

I pull out my five hundred words on the importance of James Dean in cinema from my backpack without even looking and hand it to him. Mr. Drew has a big thing for James Dean.

"Are you...okay, Zelda?" he asks a bit uncomfortably.

Good old Mr. Drew. Concerned about his students but very much *not* well versed in actually dealing with them.

I raise a hand and wave him off. "I'm good. As you were, Drew."

"Right. Okay then." He moves on.

Beth rubs my back. "It's going to be all good in the hood, babe. Don't worry. Dan won't be interested in your phone. How did he get it, by the way?"

I turn my head just enough to let her see my face fully. I'm not sure if she sees a woman at the end of her rope or a girl who has no idea what to do next, but she pulls her hand back like she just touched a disguised snake. I'm so not in the mood to describe the sequence of events that led up to the worst moment of my life, and she knows it.

Chapter Ten
DAN

The temptation *is* great, I'll say that, but I won't give in. She didn't even lock the phone in any way. And Miss Greer is known for getting so involved with writing notes on the white board that she hardly ever turns around. I have plenty of time to scour Zelda's phone. I could change all the names of her contacts to cartoon characters and still have time to take down the notes for this class.

But I don't.

If there's one thing I live by, it's honor. She did not give me permission. She was so distraught that she chased me, which makes it even more of a temptation, but it's a no-go, damn it. It doesn't matter how much I want to see her collection of selfies or how far she's gotten on Candy Crush. It'd be nice to know that she hasn't given up on the game, since it was always a silly competition between us. I certainly didn't give up.

Honor, Dan. Remember. No looky at phoney.

The bell rings for lunch, and I'm so very thankful. I don't think I could have lasted another minute with Miss Greer's back turned and Zelda's phone burning a hole in my pocket.

I'm one of the last to leave the class and, over the heads of the others filing through the door, I see Zelda. She leans against the far wall of the hall, her arms crossed, that look of "bodily harm is in your future" on her face. Sure, the assault she's planning is mine, but it's hard not to laugh.

The hallway empties quickly because food awaits, and I'm left alone with the main suspect in my future murder investigation.

She grips the strap of her backpack. "Give me my phone." Her tone is flat, hinting at the beating I will get if I don't do as she says.

Why do images of Zelda-freaking-Potts pushing me against the wall and forcing her hand into my pocket, invade my mind? Because, let's be clear, self, the girl hates us. If she did do that, it would not end the way you are currently imagining it would, and dear God, stop being such a horn dog, Garrett!

I clear my throat. "Hungry?"

I head down the hall, but she's undeterred.

"Dan, if you don't…" She goes silent, which is weird.

I turn back to her and she seems… I don't know. I've never seen this look on her face. Is that defeat?

I may be known as a heartless bastard, but her red-rimmed eyes and her chipped fingernail polish make me want to fix everything. I'm reminded of the LARP game the other night. I wanted to make everything right but there was nothing I could do. I could've yelled at Excited Julie for making Zelda protect her, but that wouldn't have fixed anything. And now, seeing her defeated? Again? I hate it. She's Zelda Potts. She's never to be defeated.

I thought I'd gotten over this. I pissed her off such a long time ago, and then again the other day, so I decided to let go of any feelings I might've had for her, because a) she hates me and b) I never had a chance with her anyway. But now that we're actually interacting more, even if those interactions seem to turn to crap rapidly, those reasons I liked her before are bubbling up. The way her bangs hang in front of her eyes so when she blinks her lashes make them twitch. And her bravery. The girl must be wearing at least four different types of patterns: flowers, plaid, polka dots... I'm not a fashion guru, but even I know that's a no-no. But does she care? Hell no. It doesn't matter how many snickers echo behind her back, this girl is fearless. And, in my opinion, that's hot. That's undefeated.

I walk up to her and hold out the phone. She snatches it before I can get a word out. "Just so you know, I didn't look at it. Except for your wallpaper. Cersei from *Game of Thrones*? Really?"

"Shut up. She's a badass." She glances at me from behind her bangs, and I think I see a hint of a smile.

"No, she's dire-wolf-balls insane."

She opens her mouth to argue, but I don't let her speak. We seem to be on amicable terms and I don't want to screw that up because of *Game of Thrones*. "Want to have lunch with me? I, uh, need some advice."

She cuts her eyes at me, obviously suspicious, as we stroll down the hall.

I want to keep things civil, but I can't help but defend myself. "Come on, dude. Why are you so wary of me? I didn't do anything."

Zelda

He didn't do anything? He must be joking, right? He's pulling my proverbial leg. He's jerking the legendary chain. He's blowing smoke up a place he shouldn't be blowing smoke up.

"You, Dan Garrett, are full of it. You know exactly what you did." I push the cafeteria doors open with a vengeance and hope they bounce back to slam into his nose. Let him see how it feels.

No such luck, though. He stops them easily. "Not going to forgive me for the basketball thing, are you?"

I have to admit that I'm starting to believe he didn't do it on purpose, as much as I don't want to. Now that I think about it, physical assault doesn't fit his style, but it is the style of the lowlifes he hangs around. Maybe they've rubbed off on him. And did he really not look at my phone? I don't know what to believe anymore.

I sit down at my usual table and look around for Beth. When I find her across the room, I ask with my eyes, *Come sit with me.*

She wrinkles her nose and shakes her head.

I give her another look that says, *Why not?*

Then Dan sits across from me and I see why she doesn't want to be near me. I lean to see around him and put on my most pitiful, please-don't-abandon-me face. She sighs, scoops up her backpack and tray, and heads my way. Loyal Beth, God, I love her.

"I mean, if you think about it, I should be the one who's angry. That stunt you pulled at the game the other night was low. Not warning me about a trap just so you could step up and get an extra chunk of experience points?" He shakes his head, and I prepare to be very colorfully insulted, but then he smiles this bright smile that's full of humor and, dare I say it, admiration. "It was freaking inspired, Z. I've seen some crazy soap opera stuff happen at LARP, but that was epic. I'm almost honored to have been a part of it."

A warning bell goes off in my head. *Do not engage. He's up to something.*

But do I listen to my brain's alarm system? Of course not. "Well, I appreciate that, but you being impressed isn't going to bring Bronla back." The warning in my head goes from bells to sirens because did I just say that I appreciate something from him? Get your act together, Potts! I go back to what I'm comfortable with, which is being an ice queen. "I didn't say I'd have lunch with you," I say as I pull out my lunch box. It's a vintage 80's Rainbow Brite one and it is fabulous no matter what anyone says.

His back suddenly straightens and he sniffs at the air. "Oh man, it's pizza day. I hate my life." He pulls out a huge, multi-level Tupperware box then takes forever opening each container. When he opens one that reeks of fish, I put a hand over my nose and mouth.

"You see what I have to put up with?" He points at his array of beige and green food with his fork. "Protein and green, fibrous vegetables. My father has lost his ever-loving mind with this stupid diet."

Beth sits next to me. "Good God, what's that smell?" She makes the question sound more like an accusation.

My mouth is full of a delicious peanut butter and raspberry jam sandwich by this point, so I just nod at Dan.

"You're probably smelling the tuna salad made with tuna and fake mayonnaise. I know, I know, it's a crime against food. But hey, *lettuce* be thankful for what we have." He uses two long celery sticks to play a "ba-dum-tiss" on his container of lettuce and spinach and smiles at us, waiting for us to get his lame pun.

My snort of laughter catches me off guard and I play it off as a cough. No way am I going to let him think he's making progress. I'm mad at him, damn it.

"That was bad, Dan," Beth says, and I do snort at that.

He shrugs. "Well, I have to laugh or I'll cry. Especially on today of all days. Freaking pizza day." He shakes his head and snaps off a bite of celery. His stupid clear, blue eyes stare at the people in the lunch line as person after person gets two slices of pizza.

I repeat the phrase "I will not feel sorry for him" over and over in my head. But it's hard not to pity him a little bit when I remember the few things he used to show true joy over. Most of them were food related. Why is he doing this to himself?

"Just go get a slice. Your dad will never know," I say, trying to show the least amount of concern possible.

"Can't risk it. I'm starting to think he has spies. I got a bag of chips from the vending machine in the hall last week. I swear, no one was around, but he knew. He lost his shit when I got home."

"That doesn't sound like your dad." I immediately regret the words. It brings up memories of hanging out at Dan's house, playing video games, eating his dad's barbecue. I remember staying up late watching the goriest, most not-safe-for-children movie at his house and both of us laughing our way through it, making pun after pun. Does that maybe make us both great subjects for a psychological study? Probably. But we loved it.

As he chews his food, his jaw slows to a stop and he looks at me. Is he remembering the good times, too?

After a slow blink, he snaps out of whatever world he was in. "Okay, maybe he didn't 'lose his shit,' but there was definitely some losing of something going on. Anyway, let's get to the matter at hand."

I take a sip of my Yoo-Hoo. "What matter?"

He leans in with a conspiratorial look. "I met this girl online. And—"

Beth's hand drops to the table in surprised shock, which begins a horrible chain of cause and effect. Her hand hits the handle of her fork, which was stuck in her potato salad, which flings the lumpy, greasy mass in its entirety up and directly into my hair.

Plop.

"Whoa," Dan says in awe. "That was like watching a game of Mouse Trap."

"What?" Beth pulls clumps of napkins from the silver dispenser in the middle of the table and starts swiping at my head.

"You know, that board game where you drop the marble on the thing and it hits the other thing, which causes the other thing to swing or something, which causes the trap to fall."

I'm about to tell Dan to stop speaking when I notice some annoying laughs coming from two tables to my left. Of course, the stereotypical jocks and mean girls are pointing at me, and they're not the only ones.

I smoosh a napkin to my head and stand. I walk calmly to the doors, back held straight. I will not let them see that this embarrasses me. I even laugh with them a little. But when I get into the hall, I run. Yes, I'm used to being clumsy, but I don't think I'll ever get used to the snickers, the laughs. They echo in my mind and grate down my spine, which has gone from board-straight to hunched, as I take a few turns and finally get to the restroom.

I allow myself a few seconds to stare in the

mirror and self-loathe. A clump of potato salad falls from my hair to slide nastily down my cheek and I don't even move to wipe it away.

Why me? I ask my reflection for the millionth occasion in my lifetime. I know this portion of my life that's dubbed "High School" is insignificant when it comes to the big picture but…it feels so permanent, so everlasting. When I go to my ten-year reunion, will everyone remember me as the clumsy girl? Will they remember me at all? Then again, who am I kidding? Like I'd ever be bothered to show up at a reunion. I'll be too busy doing… stuff and things. Or at least I hope I will.

Before I start cleaning up, a stall door opens and a girl, a senior I think, steps out. When she catches sight of me, she gives a look that makes me feel like a puny, pathetic bug she just stepped on.

Just another episode of the Zelda Sucks at Being Human show. We'll see you next week, same sucky time, same sucky place.

I keep my focus on the sink and attempt to wash out my hair. I hear the doors open and hope she left and that it's not a gaggle of girls coming in to witness my shame.

"Hi, Dan," the girl says, her voice oozing flirty vibes.

My head whips around, slinging potato salad water all over Dan's chest. He's unfazed, though.

"Yeah, hi." He's also unfazed by the girl.

"See ya later, Dan." How is she not shocked at him being in the girl's bathroom? Is there a story there? If there *is* a story there, why do I care?

Chapter Eleven
DAN

I know she doesn't want my pity, but I can't help that I feel sorry for her. I've always found her accident-proneness endearing and kind of adorable at times. But this isn't one of those times. The urge to touch her, to put an arm around her shoulders, or to simply squeeze her damp hand is strong, but just like when her character died at LARP, I know she won't welcome that kind of sympathy from me.

"Go away. You can't be in here." She goes back to splashing cold water on her hair, which is doing nothing to remove the mayo slime. I'm suddenly more angry than usual at the state of our school's funds. Can't even get the hot water fixed in the ladies' room.

I might feel really bad for her, but I won't show it, for her sake. "Fine," I say. "I guess you don't want my shampoo I just happened to grab from the locker room on the way here."

I don't even try to play out my bluff by turning around and walking away. I set the bottle of shampoo on the counter and I can't fight that urge to help her any longer. I take the elastic band out of her hair and run my fingers through her braid, separating the locks of crimson.

"Hey," she says and tries to bat away my hands.

"If you don't let me help, you won't get it all out and you'll probably end up with a soaked shirt. So just be still."

She tenses for a second, gripping the edge of the sink, then she relaxes, accepting her fate. I start by getting out all the chunks of potato, egg, and, oh God, is that pickle? Gross. I massage the shampoo in then rinse it. The water turns her hair to a nice shade of dark auburn and I'll be damned, but the silky feel of it turns me on. I try my best not to slide my hand across the back of her neck and search out stressed muscles. I have a feeling she wouldn't like that.

Well? What do you want from me? I'm a virile seventeen-year-old male. Excuse me for thinking her hair is pretty.

I turn the faucet off and grab my hoodie from my backpack to use as a towel. She doesn't stop me. Maybe she's glad I'm messing up my favorite, super-soft-from-a-million-washes hoodie. That would be very Zelda of her.

She takes the hoodie from my hands. "I can handle it from here." Surprisingly, she doesn't follow that with some insult. She pushes the big, silver button on the hand dryer and puts her head under it.

I step outside with my stuff and lean against the wall by the bathroom door. I decide to go ahead and analyze something that's bugging me. All this started out as me just wanting some talking-to-a-girl advice from Zelda and now I'm relishing the feel of her hair sliding between my fingers, and the cute way she snorts when something unexpectedly strikes her as funny. But, to be honest, it didn't really start there. She's been in the back of my head for at least a couple of years. Not that I would admit that to anyone other than myself. I try not to wear my heart on my sleeve, which I learned from Taxidermy Todd himself, so I told myself I was okay with her not showing interest/hating me.

Am I being unfaithful to effyeahFinityGirl by thinking about Zelda this way? I mean, how messed up is it that I'm having thoughts about the girl I want to ask for advice about talking to this other girl? Epically messed up, me thinks.

And of course, this moment of self-examination is the perfect time for Douchebag Donovan to stroll by on his way to class.

"Waiting to use the little girl's room, dude?" He punches me in the shoulder like we're buddies or something.

"Maybe I am. It's a lot cleaner than ours." I stand up straight and cross my arms.

The door opens next to me and Zelda steps out, then freezes, her eyes darting from me to Donovan and back. Her hair is kind of back to normal, but it's frizzier.

"Oh man!" Donovan yells so that all his lackeys beside him prepare themselves for the no doubt, super awesome burn he's about to deal out. "It's Miss Potato Head! I loved you in *Toy Story 3*."

I have to admire her. She doesn't shrink away from him. She doesn't tear up. She raises her chin and hoists her backpack onto her shoulder. "Don't you ever get tired of being a walking cliché?" Then she turns, saying, "Let me know when you figure out what cliché means." And then as she starts to walk away, she pauses. "Wait, you know what? *Don't* let me know."

One of Donovan's more quiet lackeys snickers, which earns him a scowl from the man himself. I laugh long and hard. Maybe I go overboard a little, but the guy totally deserves it.

Leaving Donovan to his douchey ways, I jog to catch Zelda. "Wait up."

"No." She doesn't even look at me, just keeps stomping ahead.

"Come on, wait." I reach her and put a hand on her shoulder.

She shrugs it off. "Leave me alone."

"Look, that guy's an asshole. Don't let him get to you." She might've acted like Donovan's childish words didn't hurt her feelings, but they obviously did.

She turns to face me and I almost run into her. She stands at her full height, which puts us almost eye to eye, but the ferocity in her stance makes me take a step back.

"Was that your plan? Stall me long enough so you could get ahold of your jerk friends so they could make fun of me?" With every few words, she tags me with that metal lunch box of hers.

I flinch, expecting another hit, when she lets out a long, angry sigh. Instead, her shoulders slump and there's that sad, defeated look again. I suddenly hate that look and never want to see it again.

"I had nothing to do with him showing up. I can't stand that guy." Why am I trying so hard with her? I obviously can't do anything right in her opinion. *Because you need her help,* my brain says, and I'm not sure if it's the truth or an excuse.

"Whatever." She turns to leave again, but I stop her.

"You wanna get out of here?" I put on a mischievous grin, one that I've seen Logan do a million times. It always seems to work on Maddie.

I must do the smile wrong because Zelda is unaffected. She shakes her head. "And let all those people think I was too much of a wuss to face them after the potato salad incident?"

"You have a name for it already? That's not good, dude. Psychiatrists say that naming a thing gives it a permanent home in your head." Psychoanalyzing her just earns me a frown. "And besides, those people might think that, but in the end, who got to skip the rest of the school day, you or them?"

Zelda

aybe being accident-prone has nurtured a self-destructive quality inside me. Like, something bad is probably going to happen at any moment so why not go ahead and get it over with? That's the only reason I can think of as to why I agree to go with Dan.

Okay, it's not the only reason, but it's the only one I'm willing to entertain at the moment.

"Are you cold? This monstrosity has seat warmers." He goes to fiddle with some controls on the dash of his SUV, but I shake my head.

"I'm fine."

It's uncomfortably quiet for a moment, then he says, "How about some music? Or talk radio? I'm sure there's some idiot on at the moment, with lots of opinions he calls 'honest' but are really just sexist or racist, that we can make fun of."

I shrug. "Whatever."

I hear my mom's voice in my head then: *Stop being a child. He's trying to be nice.* And as I'm frequently inclined to do, I argue with her. *No, he's not. He's doing something else. He's planning something.* And as she's inclined to do as well, she argues back with some little tidbit of wisdom she probably read in a romance novel, but which is actually good advice. *No one will ever be in your heart if you don't open it* is one I've heard many times.

"Fine." I agree with brain-mom under my breath, but I'm sitting right next to Dan in a quiet, enclosed vehicle so of course he hears me.

"Fine what? Heated seats or talk radio? Or music? I can do all of them at once if you want." He starts flipping switches, making the corresponding sound effects. Leave it to Dan to turn his super fancy Range Rover into the USS *Enterprise*.

My body betrays me and I snuggle deeper into the warming leather seats. "Where are we going anyway?"

"Why, the happiest place in Natchitoches, of course." He waves his hands in a broad gesture to encompass the whole town.

I panic for a second when he doesn't immediately put his hands back on the wheel. "Oh my God, will you be careful!"

He smiles at me then glances down at his knee, which can apparently steer just fine. "I'd never endanger your life, fair lady."

I roll my eyes and take a relieved breath.

Something walks into my thoughts and takes a seat. *Is he…flirting?*

"Looks like no matter how hard you try, you can't stop talking like you're in the middle of a LARP game." I find myself scratching at my nail polish again, so I tuck my hands under my thighs.

"I didn't know I should be trying to not talk that way. In fact, I try to find every opportunity to practice my verbal skills. I can't seem out of practice when Craytor returns again." He holds a fist up in the air. "Heads shall roll, maidens shall be rescued, and elves shall be insulted!"

I make sure he sees my blank stare followed by a slow blink before saying, "Right. You never said where we're going."

"The Phoenix, of course. We don't exactly have Disney World Natchitoches." He puts on an über-cheesy smile, which is way more endearing than the fake mischievous one he tried back at school. *That smile turns on the heated seats around my heart.* Oh God, did I just think that? Gross.

He nudges my arm. "Get it? Because I said the happiest place in Natchitoches. And that's a well-known advertisement slogan for—"

I hold my hands up. "I get it. Really, I get it."

I turn my head to watch a group of college

kids playing hackysack outside the local coffee shop—not because I'm interested in hackysack but because I don't want Dan to see me smile. If I could have picked one place that would cheer me up, The Phoenix would be it.

We pull into the parking lot and, as always, the blazing bird over the entrance of Natchitoches's most beloved comic shop makes these little happy vibes go skipping over my skin. When we get to the door, Dan holds it open for a couple of guys who are leaving, then continues to hold it open for me. I grind out a "thanks" and step through. His soft touch on the base of my back as he follows startles me, so I jump and look over my shoulder at him.

For a second, he just looks at me, his eyes heavy-lidded and a slight grin on his face. Then his eyes go wide and he glances down at where his fingers are touching me. He jerks his hand away, mouthing a "sorry," then gets this weird look like he's really confused about something.

Chapter Twelve
DAN

*D*ear hand, what the hell do you think you are doing? I'm hoping that scold will be enough to calm myself until I can have a good discussion with my body and how it needs to stop betraying me. Hopefully, Maddie will be here and I can sit both Zelda and her down. Once I start telling them about effyeahFinityGirl, I'm sure all randy thoughts of Zelda-freaking-Potts will leave my head.

Logan is behind the counter. "Dude!" he says when he sees me. We give each other a manly hug, slapping each other a couple of times on the back, because that's what real men do. They acknowledge the bro-love and are never embarrassed about it.

Logan's mom and the owner of The Phoenix, Martha, sticks her head out of the office and is happy to see me, too, but her smile quickly becomes laced with suspicion. She squints at me. "It's good to see you, Daniel, but shouldn't you be in school?"

I hold up my hands in defeat. "I know, but Zelda and I needed to take a, uh, personal day. High school's tough for those like us."

I hear a muffled scoff from somewhere… below me? Zelda and I both look over the edge of the counter underneath the register. Maddie is nicely ensconced beneath a shelf that holds all the regulars' bags of pulled comics. She grabs Logan's foot and he sits back on his stool before she puts him off balance. She opens a red Sharpie, fine tip, and goes to work on his shoe.

"Why is she desecrating a perfectly good pair of Chucks?" I ask, and Zelda nods like she, too, needs to know the answer.

Logan shrugs and rolls his eyes like he has no idea and he's annoyed by it, but I also see that stupid puppy-love look that means this makes him infinitely happy.

Ew.

"Cheerleader, if you could maybe stop vandalizing footwear for a moment, I need to speak with you and Zelda in the backroom." I take the Batgirl comic from Zelda's hands and place it on the counter.

"I was reading that," she says as I drag her down the hall. She stares back longingly at the comic, and the friendship bracelet on her wrist, which I currently have my fingers wrapped around, is as soft as my favorite hoodie. The whole situation makes me want to talk about effyeahFinityGirl even more because, damn it, could Zelda stop being attractive in all the right ways? I'm here to get advice on winning over FinityGirl, not to fan the fires that was—"was" being the most important word—a silly thing for Zelda that will never come to fruition.

"Please take a seat." I motion to a couple of white long boxes, the kind made for storing comics.

Maddie turns to Zelda. "I love this skirt, Zel. And you paired it with that shirt? Genius. I wish I was creative like you."

I halt that conversation before it goes any further. "Okay, fingers on lips." I demonstrate what I mean by making the *shush* gesture. I hold my finger there until they mimic me with confused looks. "I have something important to discuss with my two favorite female friends."

I should've known the "fingers on lips" request wouldn't last long with the cheerleader. Maddie grabs a stack of comics and starts flipping through them. "We're your *only* female friends, Dan."

Zelda nods in agreement. "I don't really think I'd even consider myself your friend."

My mouth drops open. "You cut me to the quick, fair lady."

Is that a blush in her cheeks? I don't think I've ever seen her blush. I didn't think she *could* blush. I definitely didn't think a blush could make a girl look prettier. Weird.

Put it aside, Dantheman. You're here for FinityGirl, damn it.

I blurt everything out before I get distracted again. "Right, so here's the thing. I've been talking to this amazing girl online and I think I want to ask her to meet."

Zelda's hand that she's using to keep from sliding off the box slips and she goes from vertical to horizontal in a second flat. But I'm close enough and my reflexes are probably the best they'll ever be in my lifetime, so I catch her upper arm before she hits the hard floor. I wrap an arm around her waist and pull her up so she's pressed against my chest. We're face to face now. I watch her eyes go all celestial again, and now there's absolutely no doubt that Zelda Potts can blush.

The thing that finally pulls my attention from the smell of my shampoo in Zelda's hair is Maddie tiptoeing to the door.

I make sure Zelda is steady before asking, "Where are you going, cheerleader?"

She freezes mid cartoon-style-sneaky-pose. "Nowhere. I definitely wasn't going to make popcorn. Definitely not doing that." She sits back down on the box with a disappointed look.

"Good, then sit down. I need your help. Like I said, I've been talking to this girl and she's great and I want to meet her, but I don't want to scare her off. So I need you two, being girls, to tell me what to say."

They glance at each other, eyebrows raised, frowns firmly in place, and I'm suddenly not so sure that this was the best idea.

Maddie leans forward, elbows on knees. "Well, first things first, who is she? What's she like? Tell us everything."

"Her name is effyeahFinityGirl. She likes all the same stuff I do, but she has her own opinions about things. She's smart and funny. Ya know, all that good stuff. There's just something about her. Like I've been waiting my entire life just to get to know her."

Zelda kind of sighs. "That's the sweetest thing anyone's ever said about…" She shakes her head like she needs to rattle her thoughts. "I mean, that's got to be one of the sweetest things anyone's ever said about anybody, which freaks me out, since you're the one who said it. But anyway, how do you know she is the person she says she is?"

"Good point," Maddie says.

"I guess I don't have any proof, but it's a feeling. She speaks like she is who she claims to be, if that makes any sense." I shrug, then point a mean finger at Zelda. "And don't think I didn't notice that slight against my honor, woman."

She scrunches up her face at me in a sort of what-are-you-going-to-do-about-it way.

Maddie thinks for a second or two before saying, "Maybe asking her to meet is a bit much. How about asking for a video chat first? That way you can get confirmation of her identity without risking the possibility of her being a serial killer or of you having a kidney harvested and waking up in a bathtub full of ice."

I take a moment to think this idea over. "That's

actually a really good idea," I say.

She scowls at me. "Also, maybe next time, don't sound so shocked when I have a good idea. It does happen, ya know?"

Zelda isn't convinced, though. "I don't know. What if she says no? Then you probably wouldn't feel comfortable talking to her anymore and you'd stop. Do you want to risk losing that?"

I pace back and forth. She's right. It would suck to lose FinityGirl. She's been there for me when I didn't feel comfortable talking to anyone else. But after she helped me with the whole thing with my dad, I have this overwhelming need to see her face, to hear her voice. "I don't want to lose her, no, but I just have to know."

Zelda

I'm so very screwed on so many levels. Dan is going to ask for a video chat and I'm going to have to say no. I haven't gotten even one tiny tidbit from him and it looks like I won't be able to continue digging. I have to fix this. Then there's level two of screwedness: the fact that I've had several moments of actually liking him today. He's been nice and impossibly, dare I say it, attractive. That hooded stare of his coupled with being wrapped in his arms, which were surprisingly strong, at The Phoenix made me want to melt into a Zelda-sized puddle. And what he said about other-me was so sweet. No one's ever said something like that about me that wasn't either a friend or family or imaginary.

Even now, as we pull into my driveway, I have to grin at how he knows every word to Allison Blair's new song "Suck it Up." When I realize I'm just staring at him, probably with a goofy look on my face, I go to open the door so I can make a quick escape. But when I unlock it, he locks it right back with one of the multitude of buttons on his steering wheel. He turns the song up as it hits the chorus and begins to belt out the lyrics, singing to me like he wants me to join him. And I swear on Captain Mal's pretty, floral bonnet, he is a horrible singer.

I refuse to join in, but I do laugh at his elaborate hand gestures. "All right, this is your car, not Carnegie Hall."

He scowls at me and unlocks the door. "In my humble, but totally correct, opinion, life isn't worth living if you're not always pretending to perform at Carnegie Hall."

I shake my head and open the door, but a quick glance at my front porch has me plopping back into the seat. "Damn it."

"What?" He looks at the porch, too, and sees exactly what.

A big box is blocking the front door.

"Must be the dryer Mom ordered. They were supposed to come tomorrow. And I don't have a back-door key."

"I'll help." He jumps out of the car before I can stop him.

"Nonono, don't worry about it." The last thing I need is to spend any more time around him, or to be indebted to him.

He ignores my protests completely, of course, because he's a stubborn jackass, and jogs up to the porch. As I approach he says, "Shouldn't be too heavy for your girly-girl arms."

I shake a fist at him. "Wanna see what these girly-girl arms can do to your face?"

He holds his hands up in surrender. "I was just kidding, jeez. I'm willing to bet those arms could do much damage. Okay, you open the door and we'll get this thing where it's supposed to go."

I move to unlock the front door, being very careful not to brush against him in any way. The other last thing I need is to turn to puddle-Zelda right now. I have to scramble and lean over the box to reach the keyhole. What kind of idiot deliverymen were these?

I feel Dan's hand lightly wrap around my free arm. I look at his hand, then at him over my shoulder. "What're you doing?"

"Making sure you don't hurt yourself. If you haven't noticed, you tend to —"

I don't let him finish. "Yeah, yeah, I know."

Finally, I unlock the door and push it open. With that done, we stand on opposite sides.

"You ready?" he asks and lifts his end of the box.

I nod and lift my end. It takes a good ten minutes of shoving and maneuvering for us to realize we'll have to unpack the damn thing to get it through the door.

Dan pulls out his keys, which have a Swiss Army knife keychain, and slices open the box. As we yank out Styrofoam and plastic packaging, I revisit the effyeahFinityGirl conversation. "So, you really want to meet this online girl?"

He grabs a sheet of bubble wrap to entertain himself while he takes a moment to think. *Pop,* pause, *pop, pop,* pause.

"Dan?" I say impatiently.

Finally he hands me the bubble wrap and nods. "Yeah, I do. I'm not one to not take action, as you very well know. I'm not going to waste time on someone who's not worth it. And I won't be catfished."

I pop a bubble. "Catfished?"

"You haven't seen that movie? Or the show?" He shakes his head like I'm so very uneducated. "Well, it's when someone starts a relationship online, but they're posing as someone else, tricking the other person. It's one thing to leave out insignificant details but it's a different thing to totally fabricate your entire existence."

I have to talk him out of this, to give myself some more time. "But what if she thinks the same about you? Or what if she has really bad social anxiety? Wouldn't asking for a video chat freak her out?"

He shrugs out of his hoodie, tossing it on the porch swing before ripping the box apart. "Doesn't matter. I mean, I'd hate to cause her distress, obviously, but… I don't know. If she is who she says she is, then this is definitely the best thing for both of us."

God, why is he so hard-headed and ridiculous and muscly and, oh my, is that a tattoo of the Death

Eaters' Dark Mark I see on his upper arm, peeking out from his short sleeve?

I catch my thoughts and shake my head to clear it. Get back in the game, Potts. "All I'm saying is maybe you should give it more time. Don't rush into this. Not only do you need to be sure, but she needs to be sure of you. You need to give her a reason to trust you. Confide in her. And remember, patience is a virtue."

He stands straight and rubs the back of his neck in thought. Yep, that sure is a tattoo of the Dark Mark. Maybe it's because I've always 'shipped Draco and Hermione, but I find Slytherins extremely sexy. He's not eighteen yet, so I want to ask how he got that very Potterhead tattoo, but I don't because I need to keep him on this train of thought.

He sighs, giving in. "Okay, you're right. But I'm putting a time limit on it. Two weeks at most."

Thank God. I can handle two weeks. I'm just going to have to up my game. It should be easier now if he takes my advice and is more open with effyeah. "That's very smart of you," I say, trying to make it seem like this was all his idea.

And it works. "I know," he says and motions to the dryer. "Now. Let's get this sucker inside."

On three, we lift and it takes a few pauses before we get the thing in its spot in the laundry room at the back of the house.

After a couple of five-minute YouTube videos on setting up dryers, Dan connects all the pipes and whatever in the back of the dryer then stands. He lifts the front of his shirt to wipe the sweat from his forehead, and I have primo seats at the ripped, flat stomach show. My own stomach does a little tumble and heat rushes to my cheeks. I try to put distance between us by taking a few steps back because this is getting too much for me to handle. Unfortunately, I trip over an empty laundry basket. I reach out, hoping to cling onto something that will stop my fall, but I grab the last thing that would be helpful. The box of laundry detergent comes down hard on my face and the white powder covers everything, including me, from the neck down. Because that's how my luck works. I might almost get knocked unconscious and covered in soap, but at least it doesn't get in my eyes.

Once I hit the floor and the cloud of detergent clears a little, I open my eyes. Dan stands above me, his arm stretched out toward me, frozen in shock. At least he tried to save me. His expression goes from shock to laughing his ass off in two seconds. I'm a crumpled heap on the floor and he thinks it's funny.

I can't help but lash out. My foot connects with his shin, lightning fast, and he buckles, his hands hitting the floor. But he doesn't stop laughing. He crawls toward me and grabs my shoulders, pulling me up.

"Are you okay?" His words are interspersed with laughs.

He checks me for injures, but I can't look away from his eyes. They lock, our eyes, and stay that way. His laughter stops abruptly. The setting sun filters in through the window, reflecting off the particles of laundry detergent still floating in the air, creating a fragrant mist that seems to separate us from the outside world, and his hands slide down to touch the skin of my upper arms. His fingers tense and his lips part. My gaze darts to his lips for a millisecond then goes back to his eyes, only to catch them glancing at my mouth, too. He leans in so quickly that I take a rapid, surprised breath. He pauses, his lips a hairsbreadth from mine.

"Z?" He's asking for permission.

For some weird, totally unexpected reason that I can't understand right now, I close my eyes and he closes the distance between our lips. It starts as a slow-moving kiss. He's in no hurry, and neither am

I because apparently all my wits, all my thoughts and concerns, have decided to take a vacation. And when his hand moves up over my shoulder to settle on the side of my neck, I'm really glad my wits decided to take a break, because this is too good.

He slants to the other side, his mouth opening just enough for him to taste my bottom lip with his tongue, and a realization slams into me.

This is my first kiss.

Chapter Thirteen
DAN

*I*t had to be done. I felt like there was no other action to take. In that moment, if I didn't kiss Zelda Potts, I'd regret it to the end of my days. My head wants to analyze the situation, but then I brush my thumb over her earlobe, and she makes a contented noise. All I can process is the soft smoothness of her skin and how her hand at the back of my neck sends chills scuttling all over me. I've had a little bit of experience with making out, but it was never like this. Those other times feel tiny and insignificant compared to this. There's electricity and heat and a need to never *not* be doing this. And amidst all the newness and fire, there's also a feeling of rightness and cool comfort. Like this is where I'm meant to be. *She's* where I'm meant to be.

I register a sound, but it's far off, not important. Then there's a voice, and Zelda's fingers on my neck tighten to the point of pain. I pull back and try to get my breathing under control, a futile endeavor if there ever was one.

"Zelda, honey, are you here? Whose car is that out front?" that stupid, interrupting voice asks from the front of the house.

Zelda's eyes go wide. "My mom."

I stand in a hurry and help Zelda up. We dust laundry detergent from ourselves and I don't really mind that I can smell and taste soap, because underneath it is the smell and taste of cotton candy.

"Zelda?" her mom calls again, this time with a hint of worry in her voice.

"Back here, Mom."

I try to look into Zelda's eyes one more time before Mrs. Potts appears and kills the mood, but she won't make eye contact. She grabs the broom from the corner and starts sweeping.

Mrs. Potts is there suddenly with her hands on her hips. "Good Lord, what happened? Oh, hello, Daniel. Haven't seen you in forever."

"Hi, um, Zelda had a spill, but we got the dryer hooked up and ready for duty, ma'am." I salute her and glance at Zelda, hoping to get a smile from her, but she still won't look at me.

Mrs. Potts takes the broom from Zelda. "I'll finish up. You two go pull a couple of pizzas from the freezer. The least I can do is feed you for helping out, Daniel."

Zelda pipes up quickly. "He can't. He's on a diet. He's gotta go anyway, right?"

"No, actually, I can sta—" Zelda pinches the sensitive skin on the back of my arm like my MeeMaw used to do when I interrupted the "grown folks talking." "Ow!" I yelp and rub the sore spot.

Zelda raises her eyebrows at me. "Are you sure? I'd hate for your dad to get upset about you breaking your diet."

Is she...blackmailing me? The treacherous minx.

I squint at her, trying to convey all my hatred. Two can play the blackmail game. "I guess you're right, I do have some homework to catch up on since we missed half—"

She pushes me into the kitchen. "Okay, well, you better get to that. Thanks for all the help. I'll just walk you out, then."

I barely get out a "Have a good night" to Mrs. Potts before Zelda drags me to the front door.

"Don't forget your hoodie," is all she says before slamming the door in my face.

I want to yell. I want to bang on the door and demand an explanation, but I don't do any of that. Can't come off as a nutjob to Mrs. Potts if I ever want to see Zelda again. And despite her own nutjob behavior, hanging out with her and having most of that time actually be civilized felt really good.

Instead, I snatch up my hoodie and stomp to my car. I pull out my phone and type out a quick text to the puzzling female herself.

Me: What the hell was that all about?

A second later, she responds.

Zelda: That was a mistake. Let's just forget it ever happened, okay?

Is she right? Was that a mistake? It didn't feel like one. When I get home a few minutes later, I'm ready to head upstairs for a shower during which I will not need to use a dab of cleaning products, but Dad calls me from the kitchen. I round the corner and Mom's there, too, chopping a myriad of vegetables, probably to stuff into next week's horrible school lunches. This does not brighten my mood.

"I got another call from your coach," Dad says as I grab a bottle of water from the fridge.

Great. Perfect. Fantastic. I completely forgot about the team meeting after school today. "Oh man, I forgot the meeting. My bad." I whisk past Dad, hoping this will just blow over.

"My bad? You can't miss stuff like that, Daniel. It's important to... Why do you smell like a flower garden?"

"I was helping Zelda put in a new dryer and the box of detergent spilled." I shrug and pray he'll respect the fact that I was doing something nice for someone else and give me a break on the meeting.

No such luck. He takes off his trademark cap and slaps the counter with it. "That's why you missed an important meeting? Because of a girl?"

"It wasn't an 'important' meeting, Dad. I bet most of the team didn't show up. I also bet their parents won't be getting phone calls about them missing, because their parents aren't crazy people. And yeah, I was helping out a friend. Is that forbidden, too? Is 'No friends' a new rule?" Sure, I don't know if I'd technically call Zelda a "friend," but he doesn't need to know that.

Dad goes slack-jawed for a few seconds, and I realize I just stepped into a Jabba the Hut sized pile of crap. I've never been very good at wrangling my sarcastic mouth.

Mom notices, too, and tries to steer the conversation away from a fight. "Zelda? Didn't you two used to hang out a lot? Red hair? A tendency to wear boots with skirts? I liked her. Would have loved to give her a thorough makeover, though."

"Layla, not now, please," Dad snaps at her, and she scowls at him. "That's it, son. I've tried to be reasonable."

I scoff at the word "reasonable," which doesn't help my case. It just earns me a tight-lipped frown from Dad.

He holds out his hand palm up. "Your phone. Give it to me. And your keys. And I'll be changing the password on the router, so no internet until you've proven you can act responsibly."

It's my turn to stare slack-jawed. He's completely, totally, utterly, horribly serious.

I tilt my chin up. My next words come from a place of desperation. "No, Dad." Maybe this is me being a hormonal teenager. Maybe this is me testing boundaries. I like to think this is me taking a stand. I feel very Katniss Everdeen in this moment.

I catch Mom's face as she looks from me to Dad and back to me. It's like she's watching a train wreck and just can't look away.

My dad wipes a hand down his face, his favorite I'm-so-fed-up gesture. "Daniel, so help me God, if you don't —" My mom's light touch on his shoulder stops him speaking.

"I don't like saying this," I tell him. "I don't like sounding like a spoiled brat, but you have no idea what these things mean to me. If you take away my phone or cut me off from the internet, I'll quit."

"Quit?" he asks.

"I'll quit the team."

Zelda

My old nemesis, conflicting emotions, tried its damnedest to worm its way back into my brain. And it succeeded briefly. For a few minutes there, I wasn't sure if I hated Dan or not. In fact, I was starting to think I might feel the opposite of hatred for him. I won't say the dreaded four-letter word because I defeated my enemy and am back in my right mind. In my eyes, Dan Garrett is once again the traitorous jerk he always was. In fact, he just added the descriptor "letch" to the long list of asshat qualities I have for him.

Not an hour after talking about effyeah's awesomeness, how he wants to meet her, and how he wants to hook up with her (yes, I know he didn't actually say that last part, but I know he was thinking it), he's making out with a girl in a laundry room. Granted that girl was me in both cases, but it doesn't matter because he doesn't know that. And I don't care how great that kiss was, or how it felt comfortable and exhilarating at the same time, the mission is not abandoned. If anything, I'm ready to get really serious.

"What was that all about?" Mom is propped against the inside of my door with a sort of suspicious look on her face.

I shrug. "No idea. You know Dan. He's weird."

She raises one eyebrow. "He wasn't the one acting weird, dear."

Oh man, I hate it when she *dears* me. It makes me feel like I'm five years old again, and I just flushed that twenty dollar bill down the toilet. That "dear" is rife with pity, a kind of "aw, poor thing, she doesn't know any better."

"It was nothing, Mom. Really."

I open my laptop, which causes Mom to sigh and leave. I temporarily think about printing out a picture of Dan so I can throw things at it, but that might come off as slightly crazy. Okay, more like licking-the-windows crazy. Instead I tick off the accomplished parts of my eight-part plan. One through four are done and done well, in my opinion. Now I just need to remain vigilant and move onto outsmarting him.

I check over the dirt—I mean, the scientific data I have on him already—but none of it is even near the breakthrough I really want. All the mean things he's said in our chats about his so-called friends seem to be stuff he has no problem saying to their faces. It's frustrating. In our chats he's called some of his teammates "knuckle draggers," he's called a teacher a "barnacle on the hull of the education system's ship," and he's referred to our cheerleading squad as, "the succubi of school funding."

Who am I to argue with all of that? I did argue about the cheerleading thing because I tried out in ninth grade, and I can say for certain that those chicks are athletes. And when I protested, he conceded the point, saying, "True. I'm not suggesting more money needs to go to the other sports. I just think more money needs to go to academia."

Damn him and his logic.

So yeah, the stuff I have on him now is kind of... silly? Nonexistent? I need more. I need something that will blow the walls off his assumed persona.

He messages me then, at the very moment I'm planning his downfall.

Dantheman: Please, God, tell me you haven't abandoned me, too?

It takes a second for me to get my emotions under control. Effyeah is the only one who doesn't know the depths of his assholeness. He's looking for sympathy, and as much as I want to cuss him out, I can't.

Me: Why would I abandon you? You of superior knowledge, you of elevated wit.

It doesn't hurt to revisit the second part of the plan as often as possible. He is a vain being, after all.

Dantheman: *polishes nails on shirt* Thanks. It's just been a rough day. Got into it again with my dad a second ago. Had to pull out the big guns.

There he goes again with trying to make me feel sorry for him. Nope, nope, and nope. I am immovable. I am an iceberg and he is the *Titanic*.

Grumpy Cat is my spirit animal.

> **Me:** Awww, that sucks. What big guns do you speak of?

> **Dantheman:** Told him I'd quit the team if he took away my internet connection. I know it sounds like first world problems, but you're kind of my lifeline to sanity, atm. Sorry if that's a bit forward, but it's the truth.

Oh lord, Grumpy Cat, give me strength.

> **Me:** No, it's cool. I'm honored.

> **Dantheman:** And in the spirit of being completely forward and honest, I feel I need to tell you something.

Yes! Is this it? Is he about to reveal his deep dark secret? Please, please, let this be it.

> **Dantheman:** I kissed Zelda Potts today. Not sure if that means anything to you. I think you and I have a connection, but I don't know if you feel the same. If you do, I wanted to be honest. If not, well, that sucks, but it's cool.

I throw my head back in exasperation, and it clunks against the headboard of my bed. I don't give a second thought to the goose egg that's probably going to form in a minute or two. This is his big, dark secret? I don't know whether to be insulted or disappointed.

Both. Let's go with both.

And what the hell is effyeah supposed to say to this? Is she supposed to be okay with it? If I want to keep chatting with Dan, other-me has to be okay with it. I think. God, I don't know. If other-me is okay with it, will that be unrealistic and make Dan suspicious?

Dantheman: Was that weird? That was weird. I'm sorry. Forget I said anything.

Crap, I'm taking too long to answer.

Me: No, I just...

I just what?

I slam the laptop closed and toss it onto the end of my bed like if I put distance between it and me that'll solve something. So much for remaining vigilant.

Chapter Fourteen
DAN

The Natchitoches Christmas Festival is weird. On one hand, I hate it. It draws tourists to our small town, and if you've ever driven behind someone who has no idea where they're going on a double-lined, two-lane, curvy road, then you know my rage. On the other hand, the Festival is our town's thing. Zwolle has their Tamale Festival—that's right, the Zwolle Tamale Festival. It rhymes. New Orleans has Mardi Gras. Well, we have that, too. All of Louisiana does. But Natchitoches does Christmas up right on the first Saturday of December. There's a parade, there's fireworks over the river, and, best of all, we get Friday off school.

One would think that having a three-day weekend while my parents are out of town for a taxidermy convention would make me happy, but I spent most of the day trying not to feel sorry for myself. It's been a week since I last spoke with effyeah. The only communication I've had with my dad consisted of grunts and shrugs. And Zelda wouldn't even acknowledge my existence once during this entire past week at school.

By the time it gets dark, I've gone through my entire anti-pity-party regimen. I've gotten five hundred kills on *Shoot Your Face 3*. I've watched my favorite Lord of the Rings movie, *The Two Towers*. And I read all of my new comics. I even order a pizza using a fake name just in case Dad has given orders to all the pizza places to not deliver to me. Still, I feel like crap so I'm desperate, which is why I turn to social interaction.

It's Christmas Festival night so there's absolutely no use in taking the monstrosity, since after the parade the roads are crammed full of families trying to get back to their homes in order to avoid the party crowd. Front Street, the all-brick road that is the center of Natchitoches tourism and runs parallel to Cane River, is not a long walk from my house, so I strike out on foot. I get to the bridge that crosses Cane River, dodging Drunky-Mcdrunkersons the whole way, and I stop for a moment to admire the lights.

Every year, Natchitoches adds a new Christmas light display along one side of the river. The water reflects the lights, making it seem like a scene from a fantasy. Lights also drip from the bridge and above Front Street. My favorite part of the lights is what I like to call the center of the web. Lights of all colors spread out in rays from a tall, old-timey street lamp at the end of Front Street and weave their way up side roads.

After crossing the bridge, I hit the epicenter of Natchitoches Christmas revelry. Front Street has been blocked off for the festival as usual and vendors selling everything from fried alligator to light-up necklaces to "Who Dat" Saints T-shirts line the riverbank. A live band is playing Zydeco music down on the stage by the water. I'm about to head there because if Zydeco can't cheer me up nothing can, but I get a text from Logan.

Logan: You should come over. Having a party. Hashtagxmasfest

One would think that with him being a total

nerd Logan would understand internet culture, but he's never gotten the hang of the hashtag.

Well, I wanted some social interaction. Logan lives in an apartment right off First Street and it's only a few blocks away. I try to cross through the festival crowd as quick as possible, but I catch a whiff of fresh funnel cake and my mouth waters. I sniff out the funnel cake cart like a bloodhound.

As I'm waiting in line for the heavenly fried dough covered in powered sugar, I hear my name boom out above the commotion. I turn to see Douchebag Donovan barreling through the crowd toward me. I want to take off, but I hesitate a second too long. Damn you, funnel cake!

He slaps a hand on my shoulder. "Dude, didn't expect to see you here. You never go out."

"Uh, I'm just getting something to eat." That's right, keep it short.

"Cool. So you know some college students, right?" he asks as I pay for my food.

What the hell? Why does he care about that? "Uh, yeah."

"Awesome. Where's the party at?"

I almost drop my precious deep fried delicacy. "How did you… I mean, uh, no. I don't know. I was just going to go back home."

"Riiiight." He draws the word out like he doesn't believe me at all, which is surprising. I never pegged him as perceptive. "Come on, dude. Don't leave me hanging. I'd love to hook up with some hot college chick." He digs his elbow into my ribs and waggles his eyebrows. "Or chicks, if you know what I mean."

I know I said I've resorted to social interaction to defunkify, but hanging out with Donovan is so not what I meant. "Sorry, man. I got nothing." I make my exit at superspeed and lose him in the crowd.

As I weave through people on my way to Logan's, I savor this sugar-covered guilty pleasure. And I don't use that term lightly. It really is guilt inducing. I know I should be feeling delightfully rebellious and I do, but my dad's disappointed face keeps popping into my head. The look he had when I gave him the "I'll quit the team" ultimatum was the worst. He was so shocked at my audacity that he just turned around and walked calmly up the stairs, into his office, and closed the door. He must think I'm such a rotten kid, or maybe he's wondering where he went wrong in my upbringing. He's probably thinking both.

God, I'm such an ungrateful ass.

I'm finally distracted from my stupid thoughts when I get to Logan's place. It's a two-story building that has about five apartments. These are nothing like those nice, new apartments they built across from the college. This place is old and well lived in. The kind of place that has seen so many Bob Marley posters, bead curtains, and porch couches, it's ridiculous. The kind of place that will never not smell like pot, beer, and incense.

All the apartment doors are open as people flow in and out of them. As I walk up the steps, I hear a loud "Yes!" from the end of the porch where a group is playing a drinking game called Quarters. Suddenly, someone punches my arm. Hard.

I turn, grasping my arm, to find out what asshole just hit me for no reason and see that I was totally accurate in the assumption that it was, indeed, an asshole.

Donovan looks around, eyes sparkling like this party is the most beautiful thing he's ever seen. "I knew you had a line on a party, dude!"

I throw my hands up. "What the hell, man? You followed me? Not cool."

"Relax. It doesn't look like an invitation-only thing." He turns to some random guy and asks where the beer is.

I shake my head as he darts into one of the apartments in search of alcohol. Taking a deep breath, I gird my loins in preparation for the dreaded socializing. I stand on my toes and try to find Logan in the sea of people, but I find someone else instead. Zelda maneuvers through the crowd with her arms drawn in and her eyes downcast. Her shiny red hair falls to the side in one of those elaborate braids that looks like it could only be done by someone with seven fingers on each hand. She's wearing an off-the-shoulder pink sweater that, on anyone else would drive me crazy because it's not straight, but on her it drives me crazy for a different reason because she's quirkily drawn a silver star near her collarbone.

It doesn't matter how many times I tell myself not to follow her, I still find myself doing just that. It feels like one of those moments when you know you're screwing up, but you still move forward.

Zelda

Beth is so lucky that I love her and I want to see her happy. Parties are not exactly my scene. The last one I can remember going to was Natalie Barten's eleventh birthday party, which I spent conversing with the moms in the kitchen instead of testing out Natalie's new makeup. And even though it was Maddie who invited us here tonight, I fully intended on not going. It was Beth's, "Come on, Z, I've never been to one of these things before. My adventurous spirit craves new experiences," that convinced me to show up.

The thing is, I said I would go, I didn't say that I would mingle or cavort or whatever it is people do at these things. So, I make it my priority to find somewhere to hide out until Beth's ready to leave.

The bottom three apartments have been designated party central and Logan lives with his roommates on the top floor, which is off-limits. A few minutes ago when we got here, we found Logan and Maddie in the bottom center apartment on the couch playing some crazy racing video game.

I wait for their race to finish before tapping Maddie on the shoulder, as is gamer etiquette. She glances up with a gleam in her eye because she just thrashed Logan and came in first place.

"Ladies! I'm so glad y'all came! Have a seat, grab a controller. You guys want a beer?" She scoots to the end of the couch and reaches into a mini-fridge to get two bottles.

"Thanks," I say and take a seat on the floor. We walked here from my house, so I feel okay about having a drink, but I should probably take it easy since, surprise surprise, I don't drink like ever. Plus, there aren't very many people here at all so I don't worry about finding a quiet place. Beth sits next to Maddie. "Thank you, I'd love one."

Logan hands me a controller. "I'm warning you now, Maddie does not take it easy on anyone. It doesn't matter if you've never played, she won't give you any slack."

Maddie shoves him playfully. "Shut up, I'm not that bad. But still, how are you going to get better if I ease up? You gotta up your game, Mr. Scott."

As we get into the game, more and more people show up. After a while and two beers, I pull my focus away from the screen to realize the place is packed and my anxiety flares. This girl needs some alone time.

"Hey, Logan, the line for the bathroom looks really long. Do you think I could use yours upstairs?" I ask.

"Sure. It should be open. Just try to be sneaky about it so no one notices you."

That shouldn't be a problem, since I feel

invisible most of the time. "Thank you so much."

I weave through people and out onto the porch, making sure to keep my arms close to my body. I slip past the loud people who've set up a drinking game at the end of the porch and duck under the sign hanging across the stairs that says, OFF-LIMITS. SERIOUSLY.

Logan hosted a LARP game here once so I know my way around. I head through the front room to the bathroom in the back. When I'm done, I figure I can hang out up here for a bit. I send a text to Beth letting her know where I am and head down the hall toward the front room to find a spot. Surely I can waste some time playing Candy Crush or something.

As I pass Logan's room, I catch a glorious purple glow. My curiosity gets the best of me. I walk in and flick on the light switch. On the wall above a bookshelf hangs something truly magnificent. Delicately, I pick up the Mace Windulightsaber replica. It reminds me of those super expensive knives professional chefs use that are weighted perfectly for precision. I take a step back and brandish the weapon at a poster of Aragorn from *Lord of the Rings* on the wall.

"Don't worry, your highness. Your Jedi escort

will see you to safety," I say in my best Obi Wan accent.

"The force is strong with this one." The words come from behind me.

I whip around out of pure freaked-out instinct, swinging the lightsaber in a big arc. It clashes with one just like it, except it's blue. I look up into Dan's smug face and wish these lightsabers weren't replicas. Sure, it's a cute face, but it's a face I'm not in the mood to deal with at the moment. I swirl my saber to move his out of the way and put the point of it to his chin.

"Don't make me slice your nose off, you scruffy-looking nerf herder." I've always wanted to call someone that, but the opportunity never presented itself until now.

He tosses his lightsaber onto the bed and holds his hands up in surrender. "I yield, but only because that is a limited edition."

He takes the Windu awesomeness from me and while he puts it back in its place of reverence, I tiptoe to the door.

"Where are you going?" I think I hear a bit of disappointment in his voice, like he doesn't want me to leave, but I'm not betting on it.

"To find somewhere quiet."

He smirks. "You came to a party to find somewhere quiet? Your logic is not quite on point there."

I deadpan a laugh. "Ha ha. I came for Beth; she's never been to something like this and I can't say no to her. So, technically I'm not at a party, I'm just waiting for a friend. Besides, I don't really know anyone here except for Maddie and Logan. It's no big deal."

"You know me. So, let's socialize. I hear that's a common occurrence at a party."

Part of me wants to tell him that no I really don't know him at all and the other part wants to say that I know him better than he could ever imagine. But neither one of those things will get me out of this situation.

I'd avoided him for the rest of the school week. If I saw him coming, I'd take detours all over the place just so I didn't have to be confronted with that full bottom lip of his, which would then lead to remembering what that lip feels like. All that hassle and all it takes are two beers for me to give in.

"Okay, let's socialize."

"Great." He claps his hands then rubs them together like he's about to start a game of chess. "Uh…"

The moment stretches out and my eyebrows go higher the longer it takes for him to say something.

"Oh! I like your star." He pokes the hollow spot between my collarbone and my shoulder and I realize that this has to be the first time a boy has ever touched me there, skin to skin.

The thought makes my cheeks warm, and I try to cover that up with words. "Thanks. I got bored waiting for Beth to get ready."

He sits down casually on the edge of the bed. "Ah, the age old ritual of making oneself aesthetically pleasing in order to find a mate."

I feel awkward standing, so I sit next to him. "Of course a guy thinks the only reason a girl would take time with her appearance is so she can be"—I make obnoxious air quotes—"'aesthetically pleasing in order to find a mate.'"

He puts his hands up in surrender again. "Okay, point taken. It's not always the main reason, but you can't argue that it's a part of it sometimes."

"I'll concede to that." I shrug and lean back on my hands.

"And I'm not saying that girls are the only ones who do it. Guys do it, too. But I'm of the belief that the physical is by far the least important aspect when it comes to attraction."

I laugh. "Oh really? So you're telling me that appearance isn't the only reason you're attracted to, say, Natalie Portman, for example."

"That's different, though. I can't help it if she's aesthetically pleasing to my eye. But she also has a degree in psychology from Harvard, so she's smart and that's hot. And yet, I know it's still not real attraction. Real attraction is different. It's not about one thing or the other or even both of those things. It's a big mishmash of a million things all at once."

I take a deep breath. This is the Dan I got used to when we were talking online. This is the Dan I used to discuss Horcruxes with over cheesy fries. The smart Dan who isn't afraid to talk about anything. My heart aches suddenly at how much I miss that Dan. But he's right here, isn't he? I want to believe that so much.

He rubs the back of his neck as he says, "Listen, about the other day, I don't know… It was…"

I hold up a hand to stop his rambling. "Let's just not, okay?" Why did that come out as so snippy?

His lips tighten and he nods. "Yeah, sure, of course. You're right. Back to socializing, then?"

I glance toward the door, weighing my options. I should go back downstairs, but it doesn't sound like the crowd has thinned out. And these last few minutes just talking to him have been nice. At least, they were up until he tried to discuss the kiss.

He must notice my indecision because he says, "Or we could watch something? Logan's roommate has an extensive anime collection in the living room."

Maybe it's the two beers or the crowd downstairs or the promise of anime that causes me to say, "Okay, sounds good," because it can't be me actually wanting to spend more time with him, right? Then he smiles, everything about him lights up, he jumps into a description of the last anime series he watched when he was here, and I am helpless.

We sit down in front of the tower of DVDs and go through the box sets. We read the descriptions out loud to each other. Most are really interesting and then some are just flat-out weird.

"Why is this guy holding a chicken in one hand and a katana in the other?" Dan shoves the case into my hands.

I shrug. "Maybe he's trained in the art of chicken swordplay? Oh! Maybe he's the hero of chickens." I put a hand over my heart and look into the distance, all concerned-like. "It's his sworn duty to protect all farmyard foul."

Dan laughs and takes the case to read the back. "Nope, wrong on both accounts. The chicken is actually the woman he loves who was cursed."

"Of course it is. Why didn't I think of that?" I

throw my hands in the air.

"That's it. This is definitely the one."

"Agreed."

While I put the show on, Dan grabs us a couple of sodas. We both sit on the couch and focus on the screen. This anime is perfect, weird and lovable. We laugh and cheer on the main character and his poultry lady. Our banter is easy and I'm having fun. This feels so familiar, but at the same time there's another layer. I'm grinning at him a lot more than I used to when we hung out. I can feel him look over at me more often than before, his eyes lingering.

When we finish the first disc of five straight episodes of *Birds of a Feather*, he pops in the next disc. He sits back next to me and I feel him looking at me again. I keep my eyes on the TV as the menu screen loads, trying not to show that my heartbeat has sped up and my cheeks feel really warm. Suddenly, he puts a finger on the star on my skin. He trails it up and over my collarbone to the pulse of my neck. "What did you draw this with anyway?"

I open my mouth to answer, but the connection between all cognitive function and my motor skills seems to have been severed.

"Wait, I bet I can guess." He leans in and nuzzles his nose against that sensitive hollow spot. "A silver

Sharpie, right?"

My eyes drift shut and I nod because that's apparently all I can accomplish at the moment. The music from downstairs is so loud it vibrates my feet, and for some reason all I can smell is funnel cake.

"I knew it." Then he kisses it, that stupid star, the product of ten minutes of boredom.

He kisses it.

That certainly breaks the spell. My eyes shoot open and I catapult to my feet.

He starts rambling. "I'm sorry. I'm sorry. Did I cross a line? I didn't mean to. I just couldn't—"

The thumping music stops abruptly, and what was a semi-loud din of voices goes up a few notches to full-on blaring. I look at the window that faces the street. Alternating red and blue lights reflect in it.

"Cops," I say, and Dan and I share a moment of panic.

He grabs my hand and pulls. "Come on!"

Chapter Fifteen
DAN

We run through the apartment and down the stairs. People scatter as we look for Logan and Maddie. I catch a glimpse of one of the two police officers coming onto the porch. Simultaneously, I cringe internally and let out a sigh of relief. I know him. He's one of my dad's good friends. He's known me since I was shitting my Pampers.

In one of the apartments, we find Logan standing on the couch, trying to get everyone to settle down, which isn't working at all. Maddie has an arm around a terrified Beth.

I turn to Zelda. "You and Beth go out the back

and head home. Text me when you get there, okay?"

Her cotton-candy-glossed lips tighten into a frown. "But what about you guys?"

"Don't worry," I say, then turn to Logan. "I'll handle this, dude."

I watch as Zelda and Beth escape through the back door, then I take a deep breath. This is not going to be fun.

The place emptied in record time, so when I go onto the porch, the only people there are Officer Warren, who I know as Mr. Bobby, the other officer, and dumbass Douchebag Donovan. Of course he wasn't smart enough to take off.

"Let's see some ID, son," Mr. Bobby says to a terrified Donovan. He's freaking shaking like a puppy. A little douchey puppy who's about to vomit.

"Hey, Mr. Bobby," I call out. "Why are you on duty on Christmas Fest night? Lose a bet?"

He turns to me, thankfully taking his attention off Donovan. "Danny, what are you doing here?"

"Well, I was about to make out with a girl, but you guys shut that down pretty quick," I say as we shake hands.

He laughs and slaps me on the back. "Yeah right, sure you were. We got a call about a party getting out of hand. Someone snuck into the neighbor's pool in the back. You know anything about that?"

I shake my head. "No, sir. Donovan"—I nod at pukey little puppy over there—"and I were just playing some video games. My friend lives upstairs. I knew there was a party going on down here, but that's not really my idea of a fun time, ya know?"

He crosses his arms, contemplating, then he smiles. "Yeah, I swear when I was at your house the other day you didn't move five feet from that Nintendo thing in the living room."

I laugh with him. "I'll tell ya, my hand-eye coordination is extreme."

"Right, well, it looks like there won't be any more trouble from this place tonight, so we'll head out, but you should get home, too. Do you need a ride?"

"Oh no, thank you, sir, but we'll walk home. Don't want to take the city's finest away from the job."

Once the cops are gone, I let Logan know everything is cool and that I'm going home. When I leave, I notice that Donovan is nowhere to be seen. You're welcome, dumbass.

I try to not think about Zelda on the walk home, but it's impossible. I knew I shouldn't have followed her. I freaking knew it as I was doing it, but did that stop me? Of course not. I can't remember the last time I wasn't in control of my thoughts or actions. Well, there was that soap-covered kiss, but...Then it hits me.

It's her fault. I can't help myself with her. It didn't used to be this way, did it? I mean, I liked her then, but I never tried anything because I knew she wasn't interested. But she's not interested now, either, obviously. I've never seen someone so repelled by my touch since I tried to hold Eliza Hamilton's hand in first grade. The way Zelda jumped off that coach when I kissed her shoulder was definitely not an ego boost. Everything was going so smoothly and I had to go and ruin it because I thought I got a vibe. So what is wrong with me?

Plus, there's effyeah. Maybe I should be concentrating on her. Yeah. If I can just meet her, she'd totally get my mind off Zelda, who I have no chance with and who seems to drive me to do stupid things.

Zelda

Beth is not exactly in the right state of mind to help me with any of my problems when we get home. She passes out on my bed the second she hits it. Mom is asleep and she has to get up early for work, so I don't feel right about waking her up.

I grab a blanket and a pillow and curl up on the couch. An hour goes by and all I've done is stare at the ceiling and think about Dan. He was really nice tonight. He's been nice ever since I started the whole FinityGirl thing. I want to be mad at him, but I can't.

I think about my plan, which was so solid at the beginning but now seems ridiculous. Did I really start this because I wanted to change things? Because I was tired of being treated like a leper? Or was it really because I wanted to take out my frustration on someone?

The truth of the matter hits me like an August hurricane. I was so mad at Dan for being a jerk and what was my response? To be an even bigger jerk. I lied to him, tricked him, all in the name of what I called science but was really just pettiness.

I should stop, but how do I do that without coming off as a total asshole? The right thing to do would be to 'fess up. But I'd lose him. Even if he does feel what I'm feeling, no one wants to be close to someone who lies to them. I'd lose this new thing that seems to be happening between us. I feel like I'm getting my best friend back. Tonight I felt comfortable and exhilarated at the same time. I don't want that to go away.

And he'd lose FinityGirl. He seems to genuinely need someone he knows won't judge him. I'd like to think I could be that person, but he'd never allow that if I told him the truth. And as tempting as it is to let FinityGirl just disappear, that secret would eat me alive.

This can't go on forever, though. Maybe I'll allow myself one last evening of nerdtalk with him. Sort of a farewell chat.

I grab my phone from my purse and send Dan that text he wanted, letting him know Beth and I made it home okay. Then I switch over to my effyeahFinityGirl account. Before, I probably would've given it some time between texting him as me and chatting with him as effyeah, but it doesn't really matter if I get caught now. I mean, yeah, it would be better if I confessed, but that's going to be a crappy conversation to have. Maybe I kind of want to get caught. I'm such a coward.

Me: You awake?

Dantheman: Yes. Can't sleep?

Me: Nope. It's been a rough night.

Dantheman: Same here.

Normally, this would be the point where I'd press for more information, but that's over now.

Me: So, question: what's your zombie apocalypse plan?

Dantheman: What a great question. I have given this a lot of thought, of course. Plan A is to go to my grandparents' house. They raise chickens and they have livestock and stuff, so it'd be the perfect place to survive.

Me: But what if the zombie virus affects animals, too? Like, what if it's airborne?

Dantheman: I don't know. How have I never thought about that?

Me: That's me. Always asking the important questions.

Dantheman: Well, I guess if it's airborne we're all screwed then.

Me: True. Okay, so it's not airborne and

let's say that you just can't get to your grandparents' house. What's plan B?

Dantheman: Board up the house, build fences, same old stuff. I've been practicing my slingshot skills so by the time it happens, I should be an amazing shot.

Me: Slingshot? Shouldn't you be practicing, I don't know, firearms or bow and arrow or something?

Dantheman: Those types of weapons will be the first thing people hoard. But do you know what section at that local Wal-Mart no one will think to loot? The toy section. And what's in the toy section? Marbles. Also, the exercise section. That's where the stretchy band stuff that slingshot bands are made of is. Knowing how to use a slingshot basically comes with the infinite ammo cheat.

Me: But can you kill a zombie with a slingshot? That seems farfetched.

Dantheman: It's a known fact that zombie flesh and bone is smooshy. You can crush their skulls with a frying pan. A marble shot by a slingshot would totally penetrate the skull.

Me: You make a good argument.

Dantheman: Like I said, I've given it a lot of thought.

I smile, knowing he's not kidding. He's probably laid awake many a night developing his zombie apocalypse plan.

I'm going to miss this so much.

Chapter Sixteen
DAN

*I*t's six a.m. when effyeah and I end the chat, so I forego sleep. Yeah, I'm exhausted, but it's that weird sort of exhausted where I feel delirious and like I could still do something. I head downstairs, looking for munchies. I'm sitting on the couch watching some early Sunday morning news program when my phone rings. The number pops up with no name. Normally I wouldn't answer, but it's local.

"Hello?"

"Hey, dude. I didn't think you'd be up." Donovan doesn't sound like his regular self. He sounds, I don't know, calm? Quiet? It's strange.

I didn't even realize he had my number. "Donovan? Why'd you call?"

He lets out a deep breath. "I just… I wanted to say thanks."

I'm shocked. I'm speechless. I'm living an M. Night Shyamalan movie. "Uh… What for?"

"Last night. You saved my ass. If I would've gotten arrested, my dad would've… Well, anyway, just thanks."

I'm not sure what to say next. I'm not his therapist, but I'm not a horrible person, either. "Your dad can be pretty intense, I take it."

"Yeah, he's kind of an asshole. I'm just trying to ride it out, ya know. It's just me and him, so once I finish high school I'm so out of here."

It's really strange feeling sorry for him. "That sucks, dude. What's your plan for after graduation?"

"I don't know. It'd be great to get a scholarship, but I'm not that smart, obviously."

"What about with basketball? You're the best player on the team." Did I just compliment Douchebag Donovan? Talk about a life plot twist.

"That could work, but when do scouts ever come to our games? I don't think that's ever happened, like ever."

I remember what Taxidermy Todd said about

getting scouts to come to our games. Maybe I need to smooth things out with Dad. And all to help one of the people I've really disliked for a long time. "You never know. I've recently learned that life can surprise you."

"Anyway, what was up with you and that Zelda girl last night? I saw y'all together when the cops showed up."

"Why do you ask?"

"I don't know. I thought she was kind of lame before, but you seem to be cool with her, so maybe she's not all bad. Do you think I should, like, apologize to her or something? Because I called her Mrs. Potato Head?"

Doth my ears deceive me? His words aren't eloquent at all, but he sounds sincere.

"Dude, that's really considerate of you. But you do realize that even if I wasn't 'cool with her' as you put, you shouldn't treat people like that."

"Come on, man, I was just having a little fun."

"That is not called fun, that's called bullying. It's mean and it hurts. You do get that, right?" I feel like I'm talking to a child.

He's quiet for a minute and I can practically hear his brain gears turning through the phone. "Guess I never thought of it like that."

I'm so confused. When did Douchebag Donovan become personal-growth Donovan? Did nobody ever explain this to him? Well, that's a parent's job and his parent doesn't sound like he's going to be winning any Father of the Year awards any time soon. Maybe the reason he acts like he does sometimes is all due to circumstance.

Huh. It's true what they say—you learn something new every day.

I try to think more on this, but my brain is having none of it. "Okay, well, you're welcome for last night. I gotta go, though."

"Cool. Later, dude."

I hang up, and I'm so done with being conscious. I'm out the second I fall face first onto my bed.

A little while later, I sit up and rub the sleep from my eyes. "Wipoo, what are you doing in here?" I ask the giant bear sitting cross-legged at the end of my bed.

He opens the pizza box next to him and holds out a slice to me. "Want some ant pizza?"

"No, thanks."

He shrugs, his fur rustling, and sniffs at the pizza that's crawling with busy, shiny black ants. "Suit yourself," he says, then swallows the entire piece whole, licking his claws afterward, one by one.

"Is Taxidermy Todd home yet?" I ask.

He perks his ears, listening, then shakes his head. "No, the evil bastard is still gone."

I guess most people might be freaking out if this were their dream, but not me. I've been talking to animals in my dreams since I was a kid. I think most people would, too, if they grew up around so many inanimate deer heads and squirrels and bears. They started out as nightmares, naturally, but that didn't last long. Thank God. By the time I was six, Mom said she was at the end of her rope. She told me that if I had woken up screaming one more time she was going to insist Dad find a new line of work. And if that would have happened we wouldn't be living the life we do today. Then again, I'm not sure if that would've been so bad.

"You know what we say about calling him that, Wipoo," I scold the bear.

He waves me off with his big paw. "I know, I know. It's not his fault, it's the guy with the gun who put me here."

"Exactly. So, how's it hangin'?"

Wipoo gives me a contented nod. "Pretty good. That was a great party last night."

"Oh yeah? You liked that? Have a good time?" Yes, I know there wasn't a six-foot-tall stuffed bear literally with me at the party, but he does travel everywhere with me in my head.

His laugh rattles the walls. Have you ever heard a bear laugh? It's loud and deep and always genuine. "I saw some pretty girls." He grins, showing off his mouth full of sharp teeth.

"Niiiice." I slap his shoulder hard. "But don't expect that to be a regular occurrence, my man."

"Aw, but it was fun. Why no more?"

Bob the Bass crawls up onto the bed then, shoving the pizza box off. He crosses his fins to mimic Wipoo's pose.

"Because," I say, "parties are just not my thing. This was an exception, since it was partly Logan's, but the only other ones I'm invited to are full of all those fake, superficial people."

Bob slaps Wipoo's leg and makes some wet bubbling sounds at him.

Wipoo nods in agreement then turns to me. "Bob's right. That Donovan guy seemed all right."

"Yeah, that was weird. It was like he didn't even know that hurting people's feelings actually, ya know, hurt. That kid's home life must be pretty messed up."

Wipoo points a claw at me. "Well, there you go."

"There what goes?"

He and Bob share an exasperated look, then Bob starts gurgling furiously at me. When he's done, I turn to Wipoo, waiting for translation. "It's not your place to judge people. Instead, try to understand them, put yourself in their place. Every person has his or her own story, and it's your job to listen to it."

Zelda

After my chat with Dan is over, I only sleep for a few hours. When I wake up, he pops right back into my head. It's a weird feeling not being mad at him. My brain is having trouble processing it. Maybe that's why it churns up another reason. He still told Martin about how I feel about sex, and the way he said it was so mean. "There's no satisfaction to be had there." What the hell? That was my business, and he had no right to tell anyone else.

By the time Monday morning rolls around, I'm back in despise-Dan mode. I'm no longer fearing telling him the truth about FinityGirl, I'm looking forward to it.

I get to school and pass Dan on the way to my

locker. He stops like he wants to talk to me but I just keep going, leaving him standing there with his mouth half open.

When I'm done with my locker, I head toward first period, but I hear him call my name. I don't even acknowledge him. I keep walking, but if Dan is anything, he's persistent. I quicken my steps and so does he. Soon, it turns into a chase. I'm trying to work out a way to my class in my head, but all solutions start with turning around. I turn left into the first open door I come to, which is the hall in front of the locker rooms. I whip behind the door and listen for footsteps for a minute before finally relaxing. I come out from behind the door and slide down the wall, catching my breath.

As much as I'm looking forward to the look on Dan's face when I tell him the truth, I haven't had time to figure out the perfect speech.

The hall darkens a bit and I look up to see Dan's silhouette in the entrance. Damn it, looks like I won't get that time I so desperately want. Now I have another thing to be pissed at him about. He made me run and I didn't even get away.

He sits next to me, our thighs touching, and I refuse to feel the spark that travels down my leg. "Okay," he says, "Um…why?"

"I don't want to talk to you. Just leave me alone."

"What did I do now? Is it because of Christmas Festival? I said I was sorry. Seriously, that was a random, crazy thing and I'm sorry, okay?"

I let out a huff. "No, it's not about that. It's…" I'm about to say the word "nothing" but it's not nothing. This is important to me. And I'm tired of not being honest. Screw the big speech. "Fine, here it is. A while back, I overheard you say something."

He raises an eyebrow, and one side of his mouth quirks up. "Oh really?"

"Yeah." I tell him what I heard and I'm sure my tone and sneer convey that I'm not pleased about it.

His brows knit together. "Who was I talking to again?"

I shrug. "Martin. But that's not important. What's important is what an assh—"

He doesn't let me finish. "Wait! I remember now. Why didn't you say something earlier?"

"Does it matter? Would you have even cared? I don't think so."

"Of course I care. Did you ever think that maybe I said that because I was protecting you? Because he didn't and still doesn't deserve you?"

I scoff. "A likely story."

"Honest." He puts a hand over his heart. "Bring me a copy of *The Hobbit*, I'll swear on it."

I stand and grab my stuff. I should say something, but I don't know how to respond. He looks up at me, waiting, and something breaks in my head. I just don't know how to deal with this revelation because despite hating him for a long time, I believe him.

I turn and bolt. I hear him call my name a few times, but I don't turn around.

I thought my good feelings about him were just a blip. I thought things were back to normal. Then he had to go and say he was protecting me. What am I supposed to do with that? I've been so caught up in getting revenge. Revenge for what, though? I don't even know the answer to that anymore. This all started out as a way to get back at him for the basketball thing, the LARP abandonment thing, and what he said about me, but I realize now that one was an accident, one wasn't something to hold a grudge about, and the other was a misunderstanding.

For the next three days, I don't have to try too hard to avoid Dan. He's actually giving me space, which should make me happy, but I'm worried instead. Thursday night, as I'm getting ready for *The Super Ones* premiere, I still haven't figured it out. I'm tired of my thoughts going in circles, so I look at Beth in the vanity mirror we're sharing. "I think I've screwed up."

"Eek, I think you're right. This wig is not sitting right at all." She yanks at the hair, trying to get it straight.

"No, not the wig, with Dan. I've screwed up with Dan."

Cara, who's been ironing Beth's cape because Beth slept in it last night, comes up behind me. "Tell us about it, Zelda."

So I do just that. I tell them about how I'd built him up to be this villain in my head and how he isn't that at all. How I feel like if I was wrong about Dan, what else have I been wrong about? Ya know, all that life evaluation stuff.

I also tell them about my fears. "And what if he asks my online identity to meet or video chat? There's no way that's going to happen, so he'll probably never talk to me again. At least, not like that anymore. He might talk to *me* me— that's doubtful, though—but not to other-me. He's different with other-me. He's more honest. He listens. I'll lose all that."

Beth leans against the vanity, arms crossed. "Okay, question number one: why would you two meeting never happen?"

"Because I'd never agree to it, of course. I thought I was ready to own up to everything, but now I'm not so sure. If he found out it was *me* me he's been talking to all this time, I'd lose him for sure. At least with maybe putting off a meeting, or just saying I don't want to, there's a chance he won't ditch me. A slim one, but still a chance."

Cara shakes her head. "If he does that, ditches you because of who you actually are, then he's not worth it. But I think there's a huge chance he won't do that. Either way, you'll have your self-respect. By telling him the truth, you'll be owning who you are—which is an amazing person, by the way—and you'll be taking a chance, reaching for what you think is unreachable. And that is a brave thing to do."

My lady crush for Cara cannot be contained any longer, so I hug her super-tight.

"Yes, my dear sister is all kinds of right," says Beth. "So, it's settled. If he asks for a meeting, you agree. Now, let's suit up!"

As I slip on my black leggings, I realize that this is exactly what I need right now. Becoming someone else, someone who's strong and self-reliant, is exhilarating. My worries melt away when I put on Finity Girl's red leotard and satin black mini-skirt.

The red mask over my eyes is the best part. I *am* Finity Girl now.

With my pity party solidly behind me, at least for the night, I get in my mom's car and drive toward the theater. The Parkway Cinema is not a big theater, but it gets the job done for a small town like Natchitoches. We even have two 3D screens. Beth, Cara, and I are some of the first to get in line. Beth looks perfect as the Bright Frenzy, with her tall, fuchsia boots and matching cape that almost reaches the ground.

As more people show up, we get asked to take pictures with them or we get questions about how we made our costumes. I've never had more fun. There is nothing better than geeking out with someone, not to mention an entire line of them. It makes me feel part of something special, which hardly ever happens. At this moment, I'm not that "weird girl." I'm a member of a community. A community, I might add, that knows how to have fun.

About thirty minutes before the box office opens, the theater's manager comes out and asks us if Beth and I want to help them by handing out the 3D glasses. Cara, who's basically become kind of our agent during this whole thing, barters for free tickets in exchange for our help. The manager easily agrees.

The excitement and anticipation of the crowd becomes almost tangible as Beth and I pass out the glasses, spouting off classic Super Ones quotes.

"As I always say, 'Go forth and be blindingly beautiful.'" Beth high fives a girl who goes to our school.

"Remember, 'True friends never falter,'" I say to Maddie and Logan when I come upon them in the line.

"Oh my God, you guys look freaking awesome!" she squeals. "The cape, the hair, and even the utility belt? You nailed it!"

"Thanks, we—" I stop speaking at the sound of a familiar, jerky voice.

"If that's what the chicks look like in the movie, I'm gonna need a barf bag or something."

I turn to see Martin Hedge, one of Donovan's lackeys and the guy who basically asked if I was easy, sneering in my direction.

Logan looks over his shoulder at him, too, scowling. Maddie puts a calming hand on my arm and says, "Did you make this cape by yourself?"

I open my mouth to answer, but Martin speaks again. "I mean, some chicks can pull off a miniskirt and some can't. Like, some just really can't, ya know? Ha! I just made up a joke: what's red and black and fat all over? That chick!"

My cheeks burn and I'm at a loss for words. Going from such a high to such a low throws off my return-insult game. I'm so used to being on the lookout for burns that I always try to have one on the tip of my tongue, but I'm not ready tonight.

"That's it," Logan says and stomps toward the theater entrance.

Maddie pats my back. "Don't let that asshole get to you."

I try to answer her, to brush off her insinuation that I care about what this guy says, but my throat won't let me speak. It's tight, holding back a sob. All I can manage is a nod and a smile. I can tell neither is convincing at all, because she tilts her head and sighs a sigh that says, *You're too precious for this horrible world.*

She puts an arm around my shoulders and I take a minute or two to get my shit together.

Logan comes back with the manager in tow.

The manager, who's a tall, burly black guy, slaps Martin on the back. "Excuse me, sir, but I understand that you've been harassing my Finity Girl. Is that right?"

"What?" is all Martin says. The girl he's with tries to defend him, but a bunch of the other moviegoers tell it how it is.

The manager whips out his phone and takes a picture of Martin. "Congratulations, you've just been banned from this theater for a year."

Of course I feel like justice has been served, but Martin throws a stink eye at me and I know this isn't over. A few people cheer as Martin and his date leave the line and head out into the parking lot.

I try to continue with my job, but every time I hand someone a pair of glasses, they either give me some type of pity comment or they kind of scowl at me. Like I'm a troublemaker or something. It was one thing to get good attention because of my awesome costume, but it's another thing to get this kind of attention.

I bear with it until I finish with my side of the line, then I leave. I don't even tell Beth and Cara that I've gone. I just text them when I get to my car.

Chapter Seventeen
DAN

It's hard to do, but I give Zelda some space for the next few days. If she wants to talk to me, fine, but she needs to be ready. I was completely truthful about everything. When Martin started discussing who would be easy to hook up with, I pretty much tuned out until he said Zelda's name. I had to think fast to get that idea out of his head.

It's a little past midnight on Thursday night when my phone dings. This is a good thing, because I was having a zombie dream, and because it's effyeahFinityGirl. The screen almost blinds me as I pull up our chat.

effyeahFinityGirl: You up?

Me: I wasn't, but I'm glad I am now. I was being chased by a zombie Kardashian. It was TERRIFYING!

effyeahFinityGirl: Oh, come on. I'm sure you could take one of them down easily. Which one was it?

Me: They're all kind of the same to me so I think my brain mooshed them together into this huge mega-Kardashian zombie. Scariest thing ever.

effyeahFinityGirl: Well, it can't be scarier than what I had to deal with tonight.

Me: Was it a Bieber zombie? I bet it was a Bieber zombie.

effyeahFinityGirl: Nope.

Wow, not even an "lol"? My Bieber jokes usually make her laugh. Whatever happened must've really been bad.

Me: What's wrong?

effyeahFinityGirl: It's nothing really. Just some jerk made fun of me. Of the costume I wore to the midnight premier of *The Super Ones.*

Me: What a jerk! Does he have any idea the time and craftsmanship it takes to make something like that? Not to mention the bravery it takes to wear it? You want me to hunt him down and kick his ass? I can totally do that.

effyeahFinityGirl: Ha-ha. No, he's not worth it. It just kind of ruined the whole thing. I didn't even stay for the movie.

I'm officially pissed at whoever this guy is now. She's been looking forward to this movie since it was announced. What kind of monster makes fun of a person's appearance? A stupid one, that's for sure.

Me: That sucks. I wish I could make you feel better, but the usual way I cheer people up is by doing my *Ace Ventura* celebratory dance. The one he does while wearing a tutu.

effyeahFinityGirl: I bet that is a wonder to behold.

I don't know why I pick this moment to ask the big question.

Me: Maybe you could behold it. Do you have a video chat program or something?

She doesn't say anything for at least ten minutes. They're some of the worst minutes I've ever had to live through, but I try not to freak out too much. It does happen sometimes. One of us will get distracted by actual real life and won't respond for a while. But right now, she is the realest thing to me.

After eleven minutes, I have to say something.

Me: Did I just overstep? It's totally fine if you don't want to talk.

A few more agonizing minutes go by and then—

effyeahFinityGirl: No, you didn't overstep. My mom just came in and told me to go to sleep. So, I'll talk to you later, okay?

I'm an idiot of epic proportions. Why did I have to get pushy and ask her to video chat? Looks like I'm just the worst at talking to women in every form and fashion.

Me: Sure, yeah. Talk to you later :)

I send the message too fast. A smiley face, Dan? Really? No wonder she doesn't want to talk in real life. I'm a smiley-facer now.

It's hard to fall asleep after that. I keep checking my phone, thinking she might have something else to say. When sleep finally does come, it's restless and filled with dreams of a blond girl who doesn't have a face.

The next day at school, I'm very distracted, to say the least, but I do notice Zelda's absence. At lunch I ask Beth about it and she just says that Zelda had a rough night. Something must be going around.

Basketball practice does not make me feel better. I sink a total of two three-pointers. No leveling-up today. Even though I'm preoccupied with my very serious problems, in the locker room Martin's voice breaks through my thoughts.

"Seriously, I wasn't saying anything everyone wasn't already thinking. But who cares, right? It's not like Parkway is the only theater around. I can go to Shreveport or whatever. It's a much better theater anyway. But this isn't over by a long shot. I'm going to get that freaky little bitch."

Looks like something is definitely going around. I grab my stuff and head for the door, but Martin stops me. "Hey Dan, you can tell your girlfriend that I meant every word of what I said. She looked like lumpy shit poured into spandex. And I'm kind of glad I'm banned from Parkway now. Means I won't have to see her in any more of her weird costumes."

I stop. The hamster running the gears in my head is working overtime to figure out what he's talking about. "What?"

"That Zelda girl, Mrs. Potato Head. She needs to watch her back." He crosses his arms.

So, last night, FinityGirl got harassed by some jerk for what she was wearing at the movies and so did Zelda. "What was she dressed as?"

Martin scoffs and looks at Donovan. "One of the people from *The Super Ones* movie. It was all red and black."

My brain-hamster collapses because he can finally take a break. I've figured it out. "Well, what d'ya know…"

"What?" Martin asks.

"Nothing, shut up, I'm thinking."

Zelda was dressed as Finity Girl. Only FG has a red and black color scheme in *The Super Ones*. The dots are all connecting.

While I'm slowly putting things together, Donovan speaks up. "Martin, dude, not cool. That's called bullying and it's mean and wrong and messes with people's minds."

My jaw drops, and I rename him in my head as Do Right Donovan.

I walk slowly up to Martin until I'm glaring down at his stupid face. "You are a horrible human being. And unless it's to grovel at her feet for forgiveness, you are not to go near Zelda or all of Hell's wrath shall rain down upon you. And by 'Hell's wrath' I mean me. It will not be pleasant. It will be the worst experience of your puny existence."

He opens his mouth to speak, but nothing comes out. Even if something did come out, it would probably be a physical threat or a curse word or a weird combination of both.

I don't give him the chance to gather his wits, though. I'm out the door, through the gym, down the hall, out the front door, and throwing my bag into my monstrosity probably before he can formulate a sentence. The Phoenix is my next destination. Maddie has a lot of explaining to do. She must've known about this. Hell, she might've been the mastermind behind it, with her always pushing Zelda and me together and all that being enamored by our interactions.

The drive to the comic shop is a blur. All

I remember of it is having a very loud pretend conversation with Zelda. It involved lots of apologizing on her part. And on my part? It wavered between being so very angry with her that I did all those stereotypical manly things, clenching my jaw, punching a hole in the wall, etc., or I would just kiss her in the middle of her sentence. And if this were a movie, a romantic comedy starring Chris Pine and Emma Stone, I'd go over to Zelda's house and hold up a boom box and profess my love for her. But that's not the case.

This isn't a movie. This is me, super pissed and wanting answers.

And even though the idea that Zelda is effyeahFinityGirl makes me feel like all is right with the world, it still doesn't make me less upset.

I pull into The Phoenix's parking lot and stomp to the front door. "Where is she?" I yell, and many nerd-heads turn my way. "Where is that traitorous cheerleader?"

Vera, Logan's little sister, who is growing up way too fast, pokes her head out from behind one of the comic book racks. "Maddie? She's not here."

"Hey, Veer. Well, is Logan here?" My original anger goes down a notch.

"Nope. They went somewhere. Dad's here but

he's in the office. You want me to get him?" She stands, carefully closing the comic she was reading.

"Nah," I say and look around, confused at what to do next. It's one of the worst things in the world, to be prepared for battle and then the opportunity is stolen from you. I'm ready to go. I have arguments and comebacks on the tip of my tongue.

Maddie must've had information I didn't. And it's so not cool that she didn't share. That's like the first thing you learn in kindergarten. Sharing is caring, damn it.

"Is everything okay, Dan?" Vera asks with the air of a psychiatrist.

It throws me off. "Uh…no. Everything is not okay."

She walks toward the checkout counter and motions for me to follow. "Let's talk."

"That's sweet of you, Veer, but I don't think there's anything you can do to help."

She puts her hair into a ponytail, like she's about to do some real work. "Let me guess. Girl problems?"

My eyebrows rise. Despite her being about nine years old, she apparently does know a thing or two. "That's a lucky guess."

"No, it's called an educated guess. My mom

taught me." She plops down in an office chair behind the counter and the contrast of her spouting some pretty wizened things then spinning as fast as she can in the chair makes me laugh.

"Of course she did. Okay, I'll play along. There's this girl who's been pretending to be someone else while we talk online. I just figured out the truth and have realized that not only has this girl been lying to me, but I'm almost positive that Maddie knew about everything." I lean forward, elbows on the counter, and smirk at her. Let's see what sort of educated solution she can come up with for me.

She stops spinning by dragging her feet on the floor and takes a second to enjoy the dizziness. "So, you came here to yell at Maddie, right?"

I nod.

"Why?"

"Because I'm pis— Because I'm mad at her." Language, Dan.

"That's fine, but I think you're acting rashly." She shrugs her small shoulders.

"Rashly? You're like nine years old. Do you even know what that word means?"

She crosses her arms and tilts her chin up. "I'm nine and three quarters and rashly is an easy word. Do you know what triskaidekaphobia means?"

I scoff. "No."

"Well, I do."

I stare at her, waiting. When she just stares back at me, I give up on learning the meaning of whatever the hell she just said and try to get back on topic. "Whatever. Why do you think I'm acting rashly?"

"Mom always tells my brothers, 'Watch where you're putting your feet.' Does that explain it?"

I pace a little. As much as I love this kid, I will not be bested by a fourth grader.

When I don't answer after a minute or two, Vera sighs like she's getting tired of explaining things. "It means think before you act. You don't know the whole story, right? And you obviously like this girl, so you don't want to screw anything up. Make a plan before you lose your temper at Maddie."

I give up being shocked at Vera's beyond-her-age wisdom. "How do you know I like this girl? I'm not even sure I do."

"You must or you wouldn't care enough to yell at Maddie first before yelling at the girl."

My brows knit together as I stare at Vera. "You're smart."

She shrugs and stands. "I know."

She leads my befuddled self to the front door

and pushes me out. "Now, go home, relax, and give the whole situation some good thought."

I'm cranking my monstrosity when I come out of the daze and realize I just got love-life advice from a nine-and-three-quarters-year-old. And what damn good advice it was, too.

Also, I still don't know what triskaidekaphobia means.

Zelda

It's one of those rare days that my mom has off. So in the morning, when I tell her I don't feel well, she's all over it. She brings me breakfast in bed—a bowl of sweet and buttery oatmeal. She asks if I want more blankets or less. She brings me some Tylenol to take for a fever she didn't check to see if I had. She just took my word for it. When she asks if I want to lay on the couch in the living room and watch a movie, maybe "play" on my laptop at the same time, I don't argue with her.

Maybe my having a shitty night then being confronted by Dan to meet in sort of real life was exactly what my mom and I both needed. The last time my mom was able to give me this much attention was eighth grade when I got the mumps. Dad had been around then, too, but he'd had to work. Despite being severely angry/depressed/humiliated about last night and being confused/conflicted/what-the-hell-do-I-do about Dan's request that we video chat, I'm strangely comfortable.

Later in the day, I'm watching *Pitch Perfect* for the twenty-fourth time (I like to keep my life statistics current) and surfing Tumblr for inspiration for the fanfic I'm working on at the moment when there's a knock on the door.

"You stay right there, hon. I'll get it," Mom says as she zooms through the living room.

A few seconds later, Beth leans over my shoulder. "Whatcha doin'?"

I quickly shut my laptop. I've been embarrassed too much recently, and the last thing I need is for her to see the newest Super Ones fanfiction I've been working on.

"Nothing. What's going on?"

She walks around and nudges my legs over so she can sit. "I brought your homework assignments. How are you feeling? Your mom said you have a fever."

Before I can stop her, she puts the back of her hand to my forehead. "I knew it! You're not sick.

No fever that I can feel."

I push her hand away. "I took some medicine. My temperature has gone down a lot."

"Yeah right. This is about last night, isn't it?"

Can't a girl throw herself a pity party without being hounded about it?

"No," I say, not making eye contact.

She taps her foot rapidly on the wood floor.

I give up lying to her because she knows me too well. "Fine. Yes, that's part of it."

She flings her arms around me. "Zelda, don't give that jerk another thought. You looked a-freaking-mazing last night and you know it."

"Thanks. I'm starting to come to terms with the whole thing. I just couldn't face it today. Plus, something else happened."

She sits up and puts her hands on my shoulders. "What? Tell me."

"Dan asked to video chat with other-me."

Her grip tightens. "And what did you say?"

I let out a long sigh and prepare to be yelled at. "Nothing. I dodged him and said I had to go to bed."

Beth shakes me and the yelling begins. "Why did you do that? You have to tell him at some point. It's like a Band-Aid—you should just rip it off. If you don't, it'll haunt you forever. Or he'll find out from someone else, which is worse."

Mom comes in then with a tray of tea for all of us. "I couldn't have put it any better myself, Beth."

"What?" I ask, almost spilling the hot tea onto my precious laptop.

"Beth's right. You need to just 'fess up and take things from there." She blows on her tea, calm as a spring breeze. "I knew it had to have something to do with a boy. You never get sick. A broken leg or a concussion I would've believed, but not a virus. And I could tell by your demeanor that this was a sickness of the heart, not the body."

"There you go again with your romance novel logic." I shake my head.

She points a scolding finger at me. "Don't discount romance novels. What do you think that stuff you write for your blog is? You call it 'fanfic' but it could absolutely be categorized as romance. Love, finding that other person who understands you, is a part of everyone's life. Some of the most beautiful and poignant words I've ever read have been in romance novels."

"Okay, first off," Beth says, "we'll talk about your fanfiction another time. Secondly, your mom is totally right. 'Fess up already."

"Fine," I spit out like a petulant child. "I'll agree to a video chat or whatever next time he asks, okay?"

Of course, there's no way that's going to happen because Dan is probably too discouraged to ask again. I'll have to find another way to rip this Band-Aid off.

Chapter Eighteen
DAN

After talking to Doctor Vera, the first thing I do when I get home is Google triskaidekaphobia, of course. Learning that there are enough people out there who have a debilitating fear of the number thirteen that they had to give it a name is almost as unbelievable as the fact that Zelda Potts is effyeahFinityGirl. *My* effyeahFinityGirl. All this time the girl that I've wanted so desperately to know better was a five-minute drive away. She was right down the hall at school and sitting in the heated seats of the monstrosity.

In my room, I turn on some Mozart and lay on

my bed, staring at the ceiling. And yes, I listen to Mozart. What kind of modern Renaissance man would I be if classical music wasn't on my iTunes? Plus, studies have shown that classical music can jumpstart the logical part of the brain, and that's exactly what I need right now. I need the emotional, hormonal, lovey-dovey part of my brain to shut up.

I don't know what she wanted to accomplish when she started this, but she probably had nefarious intentions. And as much as I want to be angry about that, I can't be too upset. I just can't. She, as FinityGirl, has been a light in the dark, a glass of water on a hot day, a 1-UP when I was down to zero lives, whether she meant to be or not. She probably didn't mean to be supportive at the beginning, but I'd like to believe that as time went by, maybe Zelda's hatred of me dimmed and she wanted to be there for me. Just like I want to be there for her.

Now, I might not be super mad at her, but I can't just forgive and forget then change my Facebook status to "In a relationship." It's not in my DNA to let something this big go unpunished. I deserve to have a little fun, seeing as she's probably been having a good laugh at my expense. I also really need confirmation that I'm right and this isn't a case of wishful thinking.

First things first, I need more information. I need a spy. And I know just the cheerleader for the job. But she can't know she's spying or she won't go along with it. I know Maddie and Logan went to the premiere last night because they invited me and I couldn't go because Taxidermy Todd said no. Even though I've been exploring my rebellious side where he's concerned, after everything that happened on Christmas Festival night, I didn't want to push my luck. It sucked on every level.

The first time I call Logan, it rings only twice before it goes to voice mail, which means he declined my call, which means he's probably with Maddie doing things I really don't want to know about. I'm not a horrible person so I give them ten minutes before I call again. And again. And again. Third time's always a charm.

"What? What? What do you want?" He sounds out of breath when he answers.

Gross.

"I need to talk to Maddie," I say.

"Then why didn't you call her phone?" I almost feel bad for interrupting them. Almost.

"Because by the way you sent me to voice mail the first time I called, I knew you two were probably…busy, shall we say, and if I'd called her, she'd never have answered because she can be very selfish. You, on the other hand, I knew would answer because you have a conscience. Really, it's not that hard to figure out, dude."

He lets out a frustrated sigh that's very loud in my ear. "Whatever. Here."

"Make this quick, Dan." Maddie sounds about as happy as Logan did, which is not at all.

I try to sound depressed. "I need a sympathetic ear, Madelyn. Do you have a second?"

As expected, she loses the upset tone of voice quickly. "Aw, sure, Dan. What's up?" She might be selfish when it comes to Logan, but she's also a bleeding heart. She once made us pull the car over on the highway because there was a cardboard box on the side of the road and she wanted to make sure some horrible person hadn't left a litter of puppies or kittens in it, which people sometimes do around here.

"I'm worried about effyeahFinityGirl. She had a bad experience last night," I say.

"What happened?" she asks.

"She went to a midnight premier of *The Super Ones* and someone made fun of the costume she was wearing. She didn't even stay for the movie. I just"—I throw in a pitiful sigh for good measure—

"I just wish I could cheer her up or something."

The silence, as they say, is deafening. She stumbles on her response. "R-really? That sounds horrible. W-what did you say her name was again?"

This should give her the proof she needs to turn her suspicion to belief. "EffyeahFinityGirl. She's a big fan of that character."

"Ah, well, that's so sad." Her voice is barely above a whisper, which means she's thinking pretty hard to figure this out. Multitasking isn't really her forte.

"Yeah, and I feel helpless, ya know?" I'm not lying. I did feel helpless when FinityGirl told me that. I feel even more helpless now. I know exactly who made her upset and I can't do anything about it without tipping off Zelda that I know what's going on. I promise myself right here and now that no matter how all this plays out, Martin will learn the error of his ways.

"All you can do is be there for her. You were there for her, right? You did listen and offer a shoulder to cry on, right?" The panic in her voice is insulting. What kind of person does she think I am?

"Of course I did."

"Thank goodness," she says on a relieved exhale.

"Why do you sound so shocked? I'm a nice guy sometimes."

I can hear her rolling her eyes through the phone. "I know, Dan. I know."

"Good. Well, I have to go." I bring back my sad voice. "Thanks for listening."

"No problem, dude. Talk to you later."

I check the time as I press "end call." It's 10:24. If I'm correct, and let's face it, of course I'm correct, she should be calling Zelda in about ten minutes. After she tells Logan the whole story.

I swear, I could rival the Black Widow in the skill of people manipulation. I'll have proof tomorrow.

Zelda

When my phone rings at 10:35 at night, I'm kind of shocked. It's pretty late for Maddie to be calling, so I hope it's not an emergency.

"So, I just got a call from Dan," she says.

My heartbeat speeds up. "Is he okay?"

"No," she answers bluntly.

I sit up in bed, my heart going ninety to nothing. "Oh my God, what happened?"

"Well, he told me something about his online girlfriend that has me a little, let's say, confused."

I relax slightly, grateful that he's apparently physically okay, but then I fully realize what she just said. My heart drops hard like the beat in a Beastie Boys song. I don't know what to say.

Maddie continues. "You're her, aren't you? You're the girl Dan's been talking to online."

Deep breaths, Zelda. I knew this had to happen at some point. I just didn't expect it to happen like this.

I close my eyes. "Yes."

It's quiet on her end for a second, then she giggles. Her giggles become louder and harder until she's full-on laughing her head off. "This is the best thing ever!"

That was not the response I was expecting. "You're not mad?"

"Good God, no. So, tell me. What's he like when he's not being, ya know, himself?"

I laugh as my heart puts itself back in place. "He's surprisingly nice, if you can believe it."

"I can believe it," she says. "Dan can be a tough pill to swallow, but deep down, he's really a big ol' softy. So, why'd you do it?"

"I don't know. It's a long story."

"Zelda, it's Friday night and this is the best thing that's happened all day." I hear someone clear his throat in the background. That must be Logan, considering her next words. "I mean, the second best. I have all the time in the world is what I'm trying to say. So spill it."

It feels good to explain the whole crazy story. How it started as this petty thing on my part, then turned into something else. How in the beginning I was holding this weird grudge against him for being popular, and how I felt betrayed by that. And now, after getting to know him, I realize how stupid that was.

I finish my tale of intrigue with, "I'm not sure what to do now. He asked if we could maybe video chat, and I dodged the question. I haven't talked to him since."

"Well, you must know how I feel about you two. I think you'd be perfect for each other. You wouldn't put up with any of his crap, and he'd probably treat you like a queen because he's not the type of guy to do anything half-ass."

It's my turn to laugh hysterically. "Yeah, right. There's no way Dan would ever be interested in me like that after this. At this point, I'll be happy if he doesn't hate my guts for the rest of eternity once he finds out."

"You're kidding, right? There's definitely a spark between y'all. Take my word for it. Anyway, I need to go, but you keep me updated on any and all happenings, yes? I have to know how all this plays out."

"Will do," I say and hang up.

Poor delusional Maddie. Her 'ship is just not going to sail. There's no way that Dan will have any kind of feelings for me. I'm *me* for goodness sake. I'm super-clumsy, opinionated, argumentative, red-haired and freckled *me*. I'm not saying I won't find that person one day. I'm sure there's someone out there who'll be able to tolerate me. But that person isn't Dan Garrett.

Is it?

Chapter Nineteen
DAN

The next day, I stroll into The Phoenix. Maddie and Logan are hunched over a comic, so she barely looks up when I speak.

"Hey Maddie, can I borrow your phone? Mine just died and I need to Google something."

"Sure." She slides her phone across the table.

I pull up her recent calls and grin. There I am and directly after me is Zelda Potts. I have confirmation.

"What are you Googling? Please tell me it's not something like how to build a spy drone because I do not want to have to clear my search history," she says when they finish the book.

I spent all morning planning out this interaction and the pay-off is going to be sweet. "I was wondering who the smartest person in the world is."

She trades a scowl with Logan, who says, "I don't think that's determinable, dude. I mean, I guess it is if you're going by IQ. But even then it's not like they know every person in the world's score."

"Oh really? Because this phone just gave me a clear answer."

"Which is?" Maddie asks.

I flip the phone around and show her recent calls list. "Me! I knew it was Zelda! And I knew that if I gave you enough hints, you'd figure it out, too. So, what did she say?"

Maddie's eyes go wide and she pushes away from the counter, rolling back in the office chair. She grabs a big stack of comics and zooms into an aisle. "I don't know what you're talking about."

I'm right behind her as she pretends to busy herself by putting out the books. "You're so transparent. You have to tell me. You owe me."

"How do I owe you?"

I throw my hands up. "I was instrumental in you two dorks getting together. Now tell me or I'll get Logan to."

She squints her eyes at me. "He wouldn't tell you."

I squint right back at her. "Wanna bet?"

We crane our necks around one of the long shelving units to look for Logan. He's suddenly nowhere to be seen. Smart guy.

"Come on, Maddie. Do a guy a favor. Please?" I clasp my hands in front of me and go down on one knee.

She hugs the books to her chest and furrows her brow.

"I'm begging here, dude. And you know I never beg. This is serious."

She relaxes her shoulders a little. "Why do you want to know?"

She's softening, I can tell, so I lay it all out. "I like her, okay? But I can't do anything unless I know the truth about why she did all this. It's a trust issue."

"Why don't you just ask her yourself?" She walks away, back toward the counter.

"Because I don't want to scare her off. And because, believe it or not, I want to be romantic and junk. Ya know, make a grand gesture."

She stops suddenly and whips around. "Awww. You guys are adorable."

I roll my eyes. "Aren't we, though? Now, please,

tell me what she said."

She purses her lips and looks at the ceiling. After a few seconds, she makes a decision. "Okay, fine. Let's sit down."

A satisfied smile spreads across my face.

Smartest person in the world. I'm going to have a T-shirt made.

When Maddie's done, I'm reeling from the information. I never realized Zelda felt that way. It's been one misunderstanding after another.

"Okay, I've told you everything. Now, call Zelda and hash this out." Maddie shoves her phone in my face.

"Uh, no," I say, pushing the phone away. "That's not how this is going to go down."

Her eyes widen. "Uh, yes, it is. I'm not lying to her about what I've told you. You can do your grand romantic gesture right now. Go on, do the thing!"

"I can't just 'do the thing,' cheerleader. I'm going to need time."

She doesn't speak for a bit, presumably because her brain is working hard again. Finally, she puts a hand to her forehead and looks down. "Fine. But don't take forever, okay?"

Zelda

On Monday, I avoid Dan like the plague, which isn't easy. He keeps trying to corner me, but I'm always quick to dodge him. He may be fast, but I'm small and good at hiding. By the end of the day, Dan has almost worn me down. I'm getting to the point where I just want to get the whole thing over with, so when someone taps me on the shoulder while I'm grabbing stuff out of my locker, I almost just blurt out that yes, I am FinityGirl, damn it! But when I turn, it's not Dan standing there. It's Donovan.

"Zelda, right?" he asks. His whole crew or posse or whatever you call them stand behind him with looks of anticipation.

My shoulders fall and I want to disappear. "Yes, my name is Zelda and yes, I know it's from a video game."

Donovan's brow furrows. "Uh, okay. Anyway, look, I just wanted to say sorry for calling you Mrs. Potato Head. I was a real douchebag and I shouldn't have done that. And what Martin did at the movies was also really bad. I'm going to talk to him, maybe make him apologize, okay?"

I don't know what to say. I'm still waiting for

the punch line, but it never comes. And it looks like his friends are as shocked as I am, because they're looking at him like he has two heads.

Finally I decide that this must be a trick. Like he's waiting for me to accept the apology before he lays down whatever zinger he's planned out.

"Um, okay. I, uh, accept your apology." I prepare myself for the upcoming burn.

"Great. So, see ya 'round." He waves bye and he's off, strutting down the hall like it's just another day.

I'm totally dazed as I watch him walk away. In the distance, Dan leans against the lockers, a smile scrawled across his face. It isn't a smug smile, though. It's more like he's listening to "What a Wonderful World" in his head. He pushes off the lockers and heads my way. And I'm super thankful that Donovan intercepts him because I really don't feel like finding a cabinet to hide in at the moment.

I turn, the fear of the Donovan situation quickly evolving into elation, and almost smack into Beth.

"There you are. Want a ride?"

I immediately say yes.

We're bumping over the railroad tracks in front of the college when she asks, "So, when are you going to ask Dan to meet?"

I stumble over my words. "Uh, I did already, r-remember?"

"Liar. I was not expelled from my mom's lady parts yesterday, ya know? If you actually had, it would have already happened and you would've already told me about it. So?"

I sigh. "I don't know. I am really ready to get it done. I just… It's confusing."

"Ask him to meet you on New Year's Eve on the river bank for the fireworks. At Julien's, that place is great. They have leather booths and those awesome giant coke floats. Oh my God, how adorkable would you two be, sharing one of those with two straws. Awww!" She smacks me hard a few times on the shoulder.

I rub the sore spot but laugh at the same time. "I am *not* going to share a coke float with Dan."

"But the Christmas lights will still be on and people will be all happy and stuff. Come on, it's the best idea ever. It'll be so romantic."

"I don't want romance, Beth. I'll be spilling my guts about how I tried to trick him. He won't be in the mood for romance, either."

She glares at me, unconvinced.

"Whatever. I'll think about it, okay? Let's go to your house and decide what we're going to cosplay for next year's NerdCon."

"Okay, I won't bug you anymore about it. And I think we need to do something with wings. I'll look amazing in wings."

Once we've narrowed our costume ideas down to fairy, gender-swapped versions of Mario and Luigi, or angel versions of a couple of our favorite fictional characters who unfortunately died in the Harry Potter books, Beth takes me home. A new chapter of a fanfiction that I've been obsessed with has been posted, but I can't seem to focus on reading it. That whole Donovan situation was very twilight zone.

I've already figured out that Dan is not a horrible person and now I have to come to terms with the fact that Donovan might not be a total dick, either. I've labeled them both as "popular," which in my head automatically meant jerks, but they've proven me wrong. There are still other people who've treated me like dirt because we're in different social circles, I assumed. But was I ever anything other than dismissive of them as well? I've never said anything nice to, say, Cindy LeDeaux. All my manners seem to go out the window when I get near someone who's considered popular.

My God, I've been so petty and stupid and childish.

Maybe it's not about being a nerd or a jock, or popular or unpopular. Maybe it's just about being.

Now, if only the rest of the school realized this.

Honestly, I didn't actually start this stupid plan in the name of science. It was revenge, plain and simple, but maybe the plan has led me to something bigger and better.

Then there's flipping Dan Garrett, who keeps invading my thoughts.

I could sit here and go back and forth over whether to ask Dan to meet or not. Or I could grow a pair.

I pull up the chat window on my laptop.

Chapter Twenty
DAN

I'm trying, really I am, but I can't seem to come up with the perfect romantic gesture. And it has to be perfect. I'm desperate, so I decide to go downstairs to ask Mom for advice. I'm just about to put my foot on the bottom step of the stairs when a bone-chilling yell comes from the kitchen. "Daniel Jordan Garrett, get down here right now!"

Since I'm Todd Garrett's son and very used to hearing his angry voice, I spin on my heel and head back up to my room. Maybe if I hide he'll think I've been kidnapped, and then turn into some Liam Neeson type of dude and focus his fury on the fictional kidnappers. Then I can plan my escape to Mexico.

Unfortunately, he's at the bottom of the stairs before I can round the corner at the top.

"Dan, what is this?"

I turn slowly, wondering what in the hell I missed. Between his thumb and forefinger he holds a small container of garlic butter that came with the pizza I ordered when they were away. I forgot I put it in the refrigerator. Like an idiot.

"I, uh…" I kind of snicker because I can't believe I'm about to get laid into for eating pizza. Any normal teenager would just apologize and go on about their business. But I think it's pretty obvious that I am not a normal teenager. I'm a fed up teenager. "You know what? I ordered pizza. And then I ate it. And it was the best freaking pizza I've ever had in my entire life."

His eyes begin to bulge and his face reddens. "We discussed this. You can't slip up. If you slip up once, you'll slip up again and again and you'll lose focus and—"

"I also went to a party during the Christmas Festival. It was a rager! There were tons of people there and the cops showed up. Now, let me ask you: which is more important to you? The fact that

I cheated on my diet or the fact that I could have been arrested by your good friend, Mr. Bobby? Because I'm not sure which one makes you more upset. And, I'm sorry, but that can't be good." I get louder as I go on. "And you know what? I—"

He stops my ranting by waving a hand, then squints at me, probably to keep his eyes from popping out of his head. "I can't believe you're talking to me like this!" He moves forward to come up the stairs, but Mom stops him.

She touches Dad's shoulder. "Let Dan talk, Todd. I want to hear this. Go ahead, honey, say what you want to say."

No turning back now. I'm banking on Zelda's wisdom. "Dad, I love you, but you're putting too much pressure on me. There's the diet, the basketball that I only started doing because you wanted me to, and the stress of getting good grades. I mean, you won't ease up on anything. You won't let me go to a movie, you won't let me even go to a LARP game, which has always been something I love to do, and you degrade it and call it a waste of time. I swear if this keeps up, I'm going to explode. I'm going to snap. Maybe I'm snapping right now."

The silence stretches, and I don't break eye contact with Dad. He turns to Mom with a confused look on his face. She just shrugs, and I get the feeling that she actually agrees with me. Dad turns his baffled face to me then walks away. I hear the glass doors to the backyard close, and I'm just thankful that he didn't slam them.

Mom crosses her arms. "Were you safe at this party?"

"Yes, ma'am. I didn't even have a drink."

She nods slowly. "Good." Then she lets out a long sigh. "You should probably go hang out somewhere else for a while. Give your dad a little time to think." The relief I feel at her words is the best thing ever.

I grab my keys and am out the door in seconds.

For a moment, I feel liberated. I feel like skipping through a field of freaking daises and stuff. With bunnies and squirrels and maybe some badass cheetahs. I've finally come clean with Dad and all I can do is hope he understands.

But what if he doesn't? How do we go forward from there? I think the only solution for the way I feel right now is obvious. Sushi.

Once sushi has been thoroughly consumed, I go over to Logan's house. Monday night is family night for the Scotts, so they're probably just finishing up dinner and are about to play some board game. Martha has gone all out this season with her landscaping. There are all these decorative cabbages lining the front walkway and the only reason I know what they are is because I used to spend a lot of the summer with my grandparents. My MeeMaw was and still is the light of my life, so I would always listen when she told me about her gardens. I could totally own as a horticulturalist.

I don't knock, I just walk in because I'm practically a member of the Scott family. And just as expected, they're setting up a game of cards.

"Hey Dan, would you like to play Nertz with us?" Martha asks as she digs out decks of cards from the junk drawer in the kitchen.

Nertz is a fast-paced multi-solitaire that can get very dangerous especially when the Scotts play. And I mean 'dangerous' literally. I've seen blood drawn and fingers jammed.

"Good Lord, no. I'd like to keep all my phalanges, please." I wiggle my fingers at her and she laughs.

Logan comes down the stairs and plops his lucky *Star Wars* themed deck on the table. "What's up, dude?"

I take a seat, leaning back on the rear two legs of the chair. "Oh, ya know, same old stuff. Just had a huge fight with my dad, can't figure out what to do about Zelda. Had some sushi. Another beautiful day in the neighborhood, my friend."

He frowns at me. "Well, that…sucks?"

"Yes, of course it sucks," I snap at him.

"Is everything going to be okay with your dad?" Martha asks, ever the caring mother, even to people who are not her children.

"I hope so. I took FinityGirl's, I mean Zelda's, advice and told the whole truth and nothing but the truth. I kind of went off, but I couldn't hold it in anymore."

"That's all you can do. I'm sure it'll work out. But what's this about calling Zelda FinityGirl?" Martha motions for me to stop leaning back in the chair.

Logan sits next to me. "It's a long story, Mom. What's happening with Zelda?"

I rub my hand down my face, still frustrated. "I can't think of what to do for her. It has to be perfect and it's driving me crazy. I'm going insane, dude."

Logan shakes his head. "Why don't you just tell her that you know?"

"She runs off anytime I come near. Besides, I want this to be big." Vera comes downstairs then, and I glare at her. "And it's all this one's fault." I point an accusing finger at her.

Her mouth drops open. "What did I do?"

"You told me to go home and think about things."

Logan turns on Vera. "You told him to 'think about things'? Don't you know what happens when he over-thinks? Bad things, that's what."

I wait for Vera to turn into Dr. Scott, but it never happens. "I didn't do anything. I just told him what Mom always says, 'Always watch where you put your feet.'"

Logan rolls his eyes. "That just means don't trip over stuff. Ya know, don't be clumsy." Vera and Martha share a look, and Logan catches it. "That is what it means, right?"

Vera opens her mouth to explain, but Logan holds up a hand to stop her. "Never mind, I don't want to know. So what are you going to do, Dan?"

"I'm never going to take advice from your sister again, that's for sure."

He snorts. "Good idea. And Zelda?"

"No clue."

"You want to know what I think?" he asks, and I nod. "Stop being an idiot, number one. Do something nice for her, then be honest. Tell her how you feel. Women do not like games, dude."

Martha goes to speak but stops. She smiles at Logan and pats him on the back. "I raised you so well."

Zelda

Step one of the new and improved plan was to find an inside man. Back in our junior high days, Olivia Rachelle, Beth, and I were the troublesome trio, the triple threat, the trifecta of awesome. Then puberty hit us all, Olivia harder than Beth and me, and her inauguration into the popular circle was quick. Even though Beth and I have always felt a little hurt by her change in friend circles, we never wished her any ill will because she tried so hard to include us. It was a weird situation. Really, it was us who shunned her. Of course, this happened long ago, and Beth and I didn't know any better. We've been civil to each other over the past few years.

Olivia and I quickly fell into an easy conversation when I called, further proving how stupid my beliefs were. She's a cheerleader and was happy to get the squad to team up with the band.

Step two was obtaining all the equipment

needed, which meant talking to Mr. Drew. I was lucky that I hit him up on a good day, meaning his rant level was at level yellow instead of red.

"Do you have a projector back there in the radio room?" I asked between classes one day.

"Of course I do. What kind of media teacher do you think I am? I have electronics of all sorts. Including the ones your Insta-twitter-chatsnap generation has forgotten about."

I wait for his rant to end because there's no stopping him once he gets going. "Good job, Drew, preserving the artifacts and all, but I was hoping to borrow the projector, maybe some speakers?"

His face scrunches up as he decides, which is weird because he has a lot, I mean *a lot,* of wrinkles and every one of them seems to be helping him choose whether or not to trust me with expensive equipment. "Okay, but I'm going to need you to grade some papers for me."

"How many papers?" Last time, when I asked to borrow some speakers for the annual Natchitoches Small Business Festival, I didn't lock down a specific number and I ended up staying late to grade papers for five Fridays in a row.

"Make it two Tuesday tests and you've got a deal."

We shake on it.

Step three was the scariest. I wanted to talk to Cindy LeDeaux. She's kind of a queen bee at school. She's gorgeous and talented at many things, including coming up with disses aimed at my fashion choices. It took most of lunch to build up the courage to approach her. Finally, just before the bell was about to ring for class, and people were milling around their lockers, I closed my eyes tight and pictured little equipment manager Colin. I remembered every cringe-inducing scene I'd witnessed that involved one person embarrassing another just because they were different. If this plan could make even one person think about changing their ways, then it was worth talking to Cindy.

"Hey Cindy?" My voice was barely above a whisper at first and she didn't hear me. I cleared my throat and tried again. "Hey Cindy?" This time it came out much louder, almost a yell.

She turned to me, her brows knitted together, and they didn't unknit at the sight of me. "Yeah?"

"I have a favor to ask you."

She scoffed. "Oh, this should be good. Go ahead."

I let out a sigh, trying my damnedest to hold onto my courage and not run away like a frightened Neville Longbottom. "Do you think you could help perform a song at the pep rally this Friday?"

She opened her mouth to deliver some prepared insult, then she paused and her eyes lit up. She's been a pageant girl since she was in diapers and to hear her tell it, it was Jesus's grand plan for her to entertain the world. "Will I be singing?"

"Yes."

"Lead?"

"Of course. No one else has a voice like you." It never hurts to grease the wheels.

"Okay, I'll do it."

And that was that. Relief flowed through me so hard.

Then the only thing left was talking to the yearbook committee, which was a breeze, since Beth is on it.

Throughout the week, I went from many highs to many lows. I wavered between feeling proud and excited to feeling downright terrified. What if we don't get a routine down in time? What if the equipment doesn't work right? What-ifs are a bitch.

By the end of school on Friday, I'm a ball of nerves.

"Are you going to puke? You look like you're going to puke," Beth says to me now as I hoist my tuba.

"No… Yes… Maybe… Probably."

"It's going to be great. Don't worry."

The students have been gathered in the gym, and the level of excitement, or rather the lack thereof, makes me think this whole thing will be a total failure. But it's too late to pull the plug.

The principal steps up to the podium in the middle of the court and taps the microphone, causing it to pop and squeal. I have to give the man credit, Principal Brockner tries really hard. He wants the student body to participate and get excited, but what he doesn't understand is that no one really gives a crap. Our team isn't anywhere near hitting the finals this year, and even in years when we did, there still wasn't that much interest from the students. During the games, the stands were populated by parents, siblings, family, and close friends. They were not full of people bursting with school pride.

"All right everyone, settle down. Settle down." And when people still aren't paying attention, he puts on his big-boy voice. "Settle down!"

The gym goes could-hear-a-pin-drop quiet, and Brockner continues. "Tonight we face off against—" The lights flicker and murmurs start. Brockner looks confused as he's led away by two cheerleaders and the podium is dragged to the side of the court.

Everyone's looking around, then the lights dim and the music starts.

It's just a voice at first, then Cindy LeDeaux walks slowly from the double doors. She hits that note perfectly and the rest of the band prepares to hit the next beat. We step out onto the court from the same door that Cindy made her entrance. Right on cue, the band sings out the chorus of a song the entire audience definitely knows the words to. It's a song that's all over the radio right now. It's about being young and going through life and just trying to make it. It's also a song about friends and being a part of something bigger.

The cheer squad makes their entrance with backflips and tumbles and confetti. The projector kicks on and Colin the equipment manager's big grinning face stares back at the audience. The drums unleash, pounding beat after beat, as the cheerleaders find a shocked Colin and lead him to stand next to Cindy. She wraps an arm around his shoulders, encouraging him to sing along. The projector shuffles to the next picture and the next in time with the rhythm of the music, each one a happy image of one of our very own students. The cheerleaders find each person in the stands and pull him or her forward even if their target is reluctant.

But about halfway through the song, people flood the court whether their picture has been shown or not.

My heart races as I play my tuba, dancing in unison with the band and the cheerleaders, and it's kind of hard to play the instrument when my mouth wants to break into a huge smile. And, as expected, Principal Brockner is just as into the spectacle as everyone else. I even see Mr. Drew up there by the projector doing a little shuffle.

The song evolves into sort of a tribal beat that's easy for even the most rhythmically challenged person to clap along with. Then we all join the cheerleaders in one of the school's most well known chants. It ends on, "We are the mighty, mighty Chiefs!" Everyone knows to stomp on the last word and it's like Louisiana just witnessed its first earthquake.

There's a tiny moment of silence, then the crowd roars and chaos ensues. I've never seen this school so pumped. Nor have I ever seen it so...together? The cheerleaders and the band line up then run at each other, high-fiving. The basketball team takes turns rubbing Colin's head for luck and he's eating it up. I really hope they win this next game because that could turn Colin into a lucky charm. Heck, it could become a tradition, making future equipment managers a big part of the team.

I duck into the hall in front of the locker rooms because as much as I love the togetherness of it all, I've never been a fan of crowds. I take a seat on one of the wooden benches and prop my tuba next to me. I allow myself some time to bask in the glow of maybe changing the lives of future Natchitoches Central students. I mean, I know this newly created sense of all-for-one isn't permanent, but it feels like a start.

Chapter Twenty-One
DAN

When I got back home after watching the Scotts injure and yell at each other all in the name of family togetherness the other night, I found Dad in his office. I asked something like, "Are we cool?" and all I got from him was a stern nod and a grunt. And that's kind of what I've gotten from him all week.

"Hey Dad, want to watch the new *Walking Dead* with me?"

Grunt.

"Did you see that ludicrous display last night? The Saints seriously need to up their game, am I right?"

Grunt.

"I've decided to join the Rebel Alliance, Dad. Do you think Grandpa Vader will have a problem with that?"

Double grunt.

I gave up after that one.

Saturday afternoon, I hear something coming from the kitchen downstairs that I've only heard twice before in my life: my parents fighting. I can't hear the whole discussion, but I do make out a few choice words from my mom. "Donkey's behind" and "stubborn mule" are very clear. A few minutes later, there's a knock on my door.

"You may enter," I call.

Dad opens the door and leans against the doorway. "Son, your mother and I just had a talk."

I snort. "So that's what we're calling it?"

He clenches his jaw and I remind myself to reel in the smart mouth routine.

"As I was saying, your mother and I understand that you have a lot on your plate. And maybe I'm putting too much pressure on you. So, I'm going to ease up because you're my son and I don't want you to burn out. But that doesn't mean—"

I finish his thought for him. "It doesn't mean that I can go crazy. I still need to be responsible, get good grades, great grades if at all possible. You'd like for me to finish out the basketball season, but only if I want to. And I'm allowed to take a break from the diet every once in a while. Did I get all that right?"

He looks down and shakes his head. Did I just make it worse? Am I about to lose any and all privileges? Or more importantly, did I just create a rift between Dad and me that will never close?

Just as I'm about to take everything back, he laughs, big and loud. "No, you didn't get it all right." He slaps a hand on my shoulder and shakes. "You're wrong about the diet. I never want to see another piece of lettuce in this house unless it's covering a big juicy burger."

We both smile at each other, and he squeezes my shoulder so hard it hurts. The gesture is not meant to be intimidating. I know my dad. It's meant to represent a hug. It's meant to stand for an "I love you, son." So, I mirror the gesture, squeezing his shoulder and smiling. And instead of saying, "Now that wasn't so hard now, was it?" I hold my tongue. Looks like everyone is making emotional progress this evening.

He leaves after making me promise that we'll catch up on *Walking Dead* later and I check my phone again. I got a message from FinityGirl/Zelda on Monday saying that she'd talked her parents into coming to Natchitoches for New Year's Eve, since they have relatives here and that we should meet. This makes the Zelda situation a million times better because now I know she wants to own up, make things right.

But first I want to do something special for her. She wanted revenge when she created FinityGirl, so tonight I plan to give her her satisfaction. The idea struck me when Logan asked me if I was coming to LARP tonight. At first I almost said no because Dad and I still weren't right, but I remembered what happened in the last game with Zelda. I've spent most of the day working on my plan and I think I finally have it perfect.

I didn't want to, but I asked Maddie to make sure Zelda was there tonight. The cheerleader will hold this favor over me for the rest of my life and that sucks. The things I do for love.

It's the usual pre-game scene at Tommy's when I get there. I'm wearing normal clothes, so a few people ask where Craytor is tonight. I give them all an automatic, "He's here. I just didn't feel like armor tonight," because I'm concentrating on finding Zelda.

She's sitting next to Maddie, hovering over a notebook, writing furiously when I find her.

"Ladies." Just saying that one word and knowing it's partially directed at Zelda causes a little piece of my existence to fall into the right place. I haven't talked to her in what feels like forever, but it's really only been days. I realize now what I was doing every time I tried to rile her up over the last year. I was trying to keep her a part of my life by any means necessary. But that tactic isn't going to work anymore.

Why did I like FinityGirl so much? Because she was everything I missed about Zelda. How could I not have figured it out sooner?

"Hey Dan," Maddie says kind of loudly, and I realize it's the second time she's said it. I've been standing here staring at Zelda with a goofy grin on my face. Thank God, she was concentrating on writing and not on seeing me act like a lovesick idiot.

"Yeah, hey. What're you guys doing?"

Maddie flips through the LARP of Ages manual she's holding. "Throwing together a character for Zelda to play tonight."

"What a fortuitous coincidence." I pull out a folded sheet of paper from my back pocket.

When Zelda still doesn't look up, I scowl at Maddie and mouth the word, "Go!"

She gives me a pleading face and also mouths, "Please let me stay."

I shake my head and motion for her to stand and get the hell out of here.

Her shoulders fall and she finally leaves.

I sit next to Zelda and place the sheet on her notebook. She frowns at me, confused. Her eyelids are covered in solid shimmer and her arms and collarbone are dusted with more shiny stuff. Her nebula-like eyes bore into mine, and when I combine them with all the glitter on her skin, she's like the galaxy.

"What's this?" She unfolds the paper.

"I took the liberty of making a character for you."

It was tough including all the attributes I wanted because you only have a certain amount of points to create a brand new character.

"I based her on you. Everything I think you are. Or at least as much as I could get."

"My physical appearance is really high…" She raises a suspicious eyebrow at me, and I just shrug unapologetically.

"So is my cunning and manipulation."

"I had to be honest. But I consider those good qualities most of the time. It takes a sharp mind to manipulate things." I catch Maddie over by Logan. He's making a pain-filled face because she's squeezing the shit out of his arm while she stares at us.

Zelda pulls my attention back to her as she reads from her character's backstory. "'Bella the elf has a history with Craytor the dwarf. He killed her sister, and Bella would not hesitate to attack Craytor on sight.' What's that all about?"

I lean back in the chair. "Just spicing things up a bit. So, will you play her?"

Her gaze wanders over the other players then back to the sheet. "Okay. Um, thank you?" I hear the question in her words and wonder if she doesn't trust me still.

"You're welcome. Have fun." I stand, nudging the manual toward Zelda so she can look up the special powers her character has, and go over to Tommy.

He looks up from his as-always thick stack of notecards. "Hey Dan, glad you're back."

"Yeah, um, I'm going to need a gamemaster right off the bat tonight for a fight."

He tucks the notecards into a big pocket on his

wizard robe. I've really got his attention now. "Oh really? You're fighting someone? Who?"

"Zelda's new character."

Zelda

My immediate reaction to Dan creating a character for me is suspicion. But I'm trying to turn over a new leaf, right? I'm not judging people anymore. I have faith in people now.

I wasn't even going to come tonight because Bronla's death was still so fresh in my heart, but Maddie was insistent.

"You can't let a character death get you down. If you don't get right back on that horse, you might not ever come back. You need to start a new character immediately," she'd said, and I couldn't argue with her logic. I came, but I did myself a favor and wore all my favorites. A lacy, cream cardigan went over my Jane Austen quote T-shirt. A navy skirt with tiny white polka dots contrasted perfectly, in my opinion, with knee-high black-and-white striped socks. Classic Converse and a rainbow scarf completed the ensemble. I twirled in the mirror, my skirt fluttering just like the princess dresses I used to wear when I was five years old and felt totally comfortable. Screw a bunch of fake armor, knowing Jane is with me is all the confidence I need.

The game starts and it seems like there's nothing special going on tonight. It's just one of those games for the players to work on the overarching plot of the season. When Dan comes over to me with Tommy in tow, I really start to regret coming. His fingers aren't crossed so his character is actually approaching mine. Why is he doing this? Why would he create a character for me that's no match for his, then add that my character would attack his on sight? Is he really that cruel? He'd have me go through a second character's death so soon after Bronla? It's the height of asshatiness.

I cross my fingers to signify that I'm speaking out of character. "Is Craytor really walking up to Bella right now?"

He nods solemnly. "Yep."

I want to run, but I have to stay true to the character. I take a deep breath, resigning myself to my fate. "Okay, I attack."

I roll the dice and get a pretty decent number. Despite the good roll, Craytor barely takes any damage.

"I take my helmet off," Dan says, never taking his eyes from mine.

I cross my fingers. "Why would you do that? It'll reduce your defense."

He just shrugs.

"Okay, that's your one action for this turn, Dan. Zelda, your turn."

I attack again and still don't do anything more than a scratch.

He removes his chest plate this time. It goes on like this until he's gotten rid of his full suit of armor. Now that he's practically defenseless, he's going to do something crazy, right? He's going to whip out some new spell he got with the XP from our big mission, thereby rubbing it in my face that I died and he didn't.

I don't cross my fingers when I ask, "Why are you doing this?"

He looks at his feet, then back at me, and his expression has completely changed. It's become something I've never seen before. Dan always has something going on in his eyes. There's always a quality of mischief or sarcasm behind them. The corner of his mouth is frequently quirked up, conveying condescension or an upcoming clever quip. But right now what I get from his expression shocks me. All I see is sincerity.

"I betrayed you, Bella. I know the reasons don't matter to you. I betrayed you and I'm sorry. Our feud has raged on for years now, but in that time I've been charmed by you. I've fallen for you. I want our anger with each other to end, and the only way that can happen is if one of us dies. Since I would rather slit my own throat than hurt you, I put my life in your hands." He swallows hard, and I feel like the sense has been knocked out of me. He's not talking to Bella, he's talking to me.

Maddie lets out a long sigh from next to me, and I realize for the first time that a crowd has gathered.

Everything has just flipped, and I can't face his sincerity any longer. I don't deserve him.

Chapter Twenty-Two
DAN

I totally *blew it*, is all I can think as Zelda turns on her heels and fast walks into the house. I look around, and everyone's face is either full of pity as they stare at me or shock as they watch Zelda leave. Maddie is the only one smiling in the entire backyard.

"What the hell? Why are you smiling?" I yell at her.

She smiles and shakes her head like I'm not understanding something.

Logan puts his hand on my back and shoves. "Go after her, you dumbass."

It takes me a second to gather my courage, then I nod and take off. I weave through players and dart to the front yard. I'm just in time to see Zelda pull away. Well, she's not getting away that easily. I jump into the monstrosity while I keep an eye on her taillights. She turns right onto the next street, and I'm pretty sure she's heading home.

I try to get her to stop because if she makes it inside her house before I can catch her, I'm done for. I flash my lights, I honk, I even call her, but she hardly even slows down and she doesn't answer her phone.

We make it to her house and she pulls into the driveway. I'm right behind, but she crosses her lawn in a sprint. "Zelda!" I call as I reach the door right as she slams it behind her. "Zelda, come on! Talk to me, please!" I bang on the door and wait, but there's no answer.

I'm about to bang again when the door thankfully opens. Mrs. Potts stands there.

"Um, good evening, I was wondering if I could speak to Zelda?"

She looks down the hall then back at me. "She said to let you in, but—"

I don't allow her to finish, which is rude, I know, but I have to press my advantage. "Please, Mrs.

Potts. I just want to talk to her and make sure she's all right."

She stares me down for a second then takes a cautious step back to let me in. I make it down the hall to Zelda's room and peek in. I find her on the floor by her bed, her computer in her lap.

"Z?"

She looks up, and it hurts so much to see her cheeks damp with tears. I sit down next to her, and that impulsiveness that she stirs in me takes control. I wrap an arm around her and her head falls onto my shoulder. I wait and wait and not once do I get impatient. If it were up to me, I could sit right here like this with her for years. Ya know, as long as people brought us some Hot Pockets and apple juice every once in a while.

Soon, she gets her breathing under control and sits up. "I can't lie to you anymore. Here's the truth. I'm effyeahFinityGirl and I did it so I could get back at you for being a jerk and now I realize you aren't the jerk I thought you were. I mean, you can be a jerk, but not too bad, and definitely not as big of a jerk as I can apparently be and just... Here."

She turns the laptop so I can see what she's pulled up. There are tons of screen captures of our chats. Every instance I was even the tiniest bit insulting to anyone, she caught it. Clever girl.

I close the laptop and put it on the bed behind us. "I don't care."

She blinks a few times out of shock, causing another tear to roll down her cheek. "What? How can you not care? I've been tricking you for weeks and you don't care?"

I shrug. "Well, technically, you weren't tricking me for as long as you think you were. I've known for a while."

She leans away from me, her expression slowly transforming from shock to disgust. Then she slaps my chest so hard that I know I'll have a Zelda-hand-shaped red mark there for at least a few hours.

Zelda

"How long have you known?" How long has he let me live with this guilt? How long did he allow me to suffer?

He scoots about three feet away, rubbing his chest. "Since the day after *The Super Ones* premiere."

That was a week ago. He let me feel horrible for a whole week. "Why didn't you say anything?"

He straightens, his chin tilting up a little. "It's like Wipoo said—"

"Who the hell is Wipoo?"

"The big bear in my living room?" He speaks fast, exasperated at having to explain. "He was a bear, like Winnie the Pooh, I was like three and couldn't get all the syllables in there, hence Wipoo. I dream about him sometimes. Anyway, he and Bob—"

I throw my hands up. "Who the hell is—"

"It doesn't matter! They said that every person has a story and it's my job to listen to it. I didn't want to scare you off. I wanted you to come to me. I wanted to hear your story. But I couldn't wait any longer. But that's okay because the story isn't over yet. Our story is just beginning."

I see that usual twinkle of mischief in his eyes. "How long did it take you to come up with that little speech?"

He smiles. "Like most of second period on Thursday."

I wipe at my tears and let a laugh escape.

Everything turns into a happy blur as he leans in, then grabs my face. I wrap an arm around his neck and pull him into a kiss that's like our first, comfortable and exhilarating, but there's something new about it, too. I relish the feel of his lips on mine. They're cool and smooth and everything I want in this quick second. Then I realize what's new: trust.

I totally trust him when we slide all the way to the floor. I trust him when he interlocks our fingers then brings them to his mouth for a quick peck. I continue to trust him for the next good fifteen minutes of his mouth on mine.

There's a loud bang, causing us to jump.

"Holy shhhh," Dan says and looks around.

My mom's voice causes my cheeks to heat up even more. "Don't mind me. Just doing the dishes. Here. In the kitchen. Because I'm still here and stuff."

I laugh a little, and he smiles. He takes my hand.

"Want to go back to the game? If we don't tell the cheerleader that everything is okay, she'll start calling and won't stop until we pick up."

I nod. "Good idea, but I have one more question."

He rubs a hand over his face. "Dear Lord in heaven, what is it?"

"Who's Bob?"

Epilogue
Zelda

FEBRUARY 13TH

I've always thought Valentine's Day was just a corporate scheme to get us to buy more crap, but I kind of get it now. It's nice to look forward to that special day when you're supposed to let those whom you love know it. Then again, we should be doing that every day, right?

Whatever. I like chocolate.

I wasn't expecting Dan to want to go tonight. Hell, I didn't expect to want to go myself, but when he asked me, I grinned and got a silly zing in my stomach. I couldn't say no.

I've never been to a school dance before and I'm trying to do this one up right. Cara designed and sewed my dress. It's black and white polka-dotted with a sweetheart neckline and a butt-ton of red toile under the skirt. I made my own pair of ruby slippers using some cheap satin shoes, spray glue, and an entire bottle of red glitter. Don't judge me. I'm a big *Wizard of Oz* fan, okay?

My mom did my makeup, giving me sleek black eyeliner and a classic red lip. My nails are a sparkly red to match my shoes and my hair is very mermaid-ish, down and perfectly wavy.

"If Daniel doesn't pass out due to your beauty, he's insane," Mom says as we look in a full-length mirror in the bathroom.

I glance over my shoulder at her. "Sounds like someone's been working on her latest novel."

She shrugs and smiles. "It's a nice way to pass the time."

I'm super proud of her. She's been writing like a madwoman these past few weeks. She loves it and she's really good at it. "Those chapters you gave me the other day didn't seem like just a pastime. I might have to take back some of the things I've said about those books. Just do me a favor and keep the sex stuff to yourself, okay? I'd rather not be scarred for life."

She shivers dramatically. "Yeah, there's no way you're reading that."

I put on the final touch, which is a spritz of perfume, and all I need now is my date.

DAN

"This is pitiful. You realize this, right, Dad?" I ask.

He concentrates on the video playing on his tablet, which he's watched about five times. "We can do this. It can't be that difficult."

"Why don't we just call Mom? I bet—"

He holds up a hand and gives me a stern look. "Absolutely not. Let me try again."

Mom comes into my room then, and I let out a relieved sigh. "Give it to me," she says.

"I've got this, Layla." Dad holds the object of our frustration out of her reach.

She shakes her head. "Why don't you just borrow one of your dad's ties, Daniel? I'm sure you can tie one of those."

"Nope," I say for millionth time. "It has to be a bowtie."

"Why?" Dad whines.

"Because bowties are cool."

After a couple more tries, we finally get it perfect. The red bowtie looks great with my black suit and, from what Beth told me, Zelda and I should match. I mean, that's what couples are supposed to do at these things, right?

Couple. The word still throws me for a loop when I think about it in connection to Zelda and me. We've been together a little over a month and it's been kind of the best month of my life. I know it sounds cliché, something I've strived to never be, but I gave up that ghost the second I saw her reaction to the belated Christmas present I got her.

She was a little confused when we drove to my MeeMaw's house, which is farther out in the country. I'd spent hours at Kaffie-Fredricks general store looking for the right one, so I wanted to have as much space as possible for the first time she used it. When she pulled the glossy, wooden slingshot out of the zombie-themed bag, the smile that lit up her face was a freaking vision. I instantly regretted all that time I'd spent trying to rile her up just so I could see vibrant fury in her eyes. This smile was glorious, a million times better. We spent the day practicing shooting bottles and cans. I'm almost ashamed to admit that by the time we left, she had better aim than I did.

That day super confirmed that making her happy made me happy, and when I find something that makes me happy, be it video games or comics or being the cause of Zelda's smile, then I go at it full force. And that's why I'm attending this dance. Plus, there are still a few girls who won't leave me alone. I have to pull Zelda close every time we're together at school in hopes of sending a message to Carrie Danvers that I am off the market.

Okay, maybe I don't *have* to pull Z close. A simple arm around the shoulders or holding her hand might do the trick, but I like to hear her soft sigh when I plant a kiss on the top of her head.

Zelda

Dan's parents arrive at my house before he does. Normally, I'd be pretty uncomfortable with all this fuss, but I'm getting used to receiving positive attention. That's all Dan's doing. Maddie was so right when she said that he'd be a great boyfriend because he doesn't do anything half-ass.

I see his "go big or go home" attitude hasn't slacked at all when he gets here. He looks super handsome in a black suit and red bowtie. He's even styled his wavy hair. His dad is straightening his bowtie when I step out onto the lawn and he turns in my direction. I don't think I've ever been ogled before. If I have been, I didn't know it. Now, I feel completely and utterly ogled. In a good way.

He smiles and offers me his arm. When I take it, he whispers, "'Hear my soul speak. Of the very instant that I saw you, did my heart fly at your service.'"

My mouth drops open. He finally got a quote right. "How long have you been planning to say that?"

"Can't get anything past you, can I? One of these days, you're going to have to give me some slack."

I let out an evil chuckle. "Never. So, how long?"

He goes to run a hand through his hair, but I stop him so he doesn't mess up the perfect disheveled-ness of it. "Since the day after I asked you, okay? People talk about how romantic Shakespeare was, but most of his comments on love and beauty are pretty depressing."

I nod in agreement.

We can't say much else because the parents want their photoshoot. We do all the standard poses, then he runs to the monstrosity. When he comes back, he has a couple of props in hand.

"Now we can do a couple of shots that I will actually frame and put up in my room." He hands me a purple lightsaber and he brandishes his own blue one.

We do combat pose after combat pose, but I think my favorite one will be where we're pretending that I'm pulling a Darth Vader force-choke on him.

When we're done, Mom stops me before we leave. She does those mom things like patting my shoulders and fixing my hair even though it probably doesn't need fixing. "Have fun, honey. Be safe. I trust you. Be good."

I stop her just as tears well up in her eyes. "Mom, it's just a Valentine's dance. This isn't prom or my wedding day or anything."

"I know. Just… Be careful, okay?"

I ease up on her. "We will, Mom. I'll call you. Love you."

I hop in the car with Dan, he turns on the heated seats, and we're off.

IF YOU LOVED ROMANCING THE NERD, YOU WON'T WANT TO MISS LOGAN AND MADDIE'S STORY IN

AVAILABLE IN STORES AND ONLINE NOW!

Acknowledgments

Thanks to the entire Entangled crew. Thanks to Heather Howland for liking Dan enough to want to hear more of his crazy. Thanks to Stacy Abrams for her wisdom and patience, especially the patience. Thanks to my agent, Jenny Bent, for taking me on and for being all-around awesome.

Thanks to my family for all the advice and for putting up with me during the process. Mom, thanks for cooking for me when I was feeling down and always being there to listen to me rant. Brian, thanks for the same reason. Caleb, thanks for never letting me go without seeing actual people for too long.

Thanks to Stefanie Gaither, who is the best JHFP critique partner, but an even better friend. Thanks to Kayti McGee for the midnight chats and the constant encouragement. Thanks to Ashley Fuller for having beautiful hair and for being awesomely noir. Thanks to Lauralin Paige and Bethany Hagan for that great reading in Savannah; it really helped me see things in a new way. Thanks to Melinda Beatty, Nicole Zoltack, HE Griffin, Amber Tuscan-Clites, Melanie Harlow, and Gennifer Albin for being such lovely retreat buddies.

A huge thank-you to the fans of *The Summer I Became a Nerd.* Your frequent emails, tweets, and other posts got me through so many hard days. This book would never have happened without you guys.

Thanks to my sons, Tommy and Lucas, for the constant reminders to "do work" and the always available cuddles.

Finally, thank you to my husband, Shane Miller. You never let me give up, you were always there with a pep talk, and you listened to me babble even when you'd heard it all before. I'm the luckiest wife in the world, basically. I love you.

CHECK OUT MORE OF ENTANGLED TEEN'S HOTTEST READS...

WHATEVER LIFE THROWS AT YOU BY JULIE CROSS

When seventeen-year-old track star Annie Lucas's dad starts mentoring nineteen-year-old baseball rookie phenom, Jason Brody, Annie's convinced she knows his type—arrogant, bossy, and most likely not into high school girls. But as Brody and her father grow closer, Annie starts to see through his façade to the lonely boy in over his head. When opening day comes around and her dad—and Brody's—job is on the line, she's reminded why he's off-limits. But Brody needs her, and staying away isn't an option.

PAPER OR PLASTIC

BY VIVI BARNES

Busted. Lexie Dubois just got caught shoplifting a cheap tube of lipstick at the SmartMart.

And her punishment is spending her summer working at the weird cheap-o store, where the only thing stranger than customers are the staff. Coupon cutters, jerk customers, and learning exactly what a "Code B" really is (ew). And for added awkwardness, her new supervisor is the very cute—and least popular guy in school—Noah Grayson. And this summer, she'll learn there's a whole lot more to SmartMart than she ever imagined...

Life Unaware
by Cole Gibsen

Regan Flay is following her control-freak mother's "plan" for high school success, until everything goes horribly wrong. Every bitchy text or email is printed out and taped to every locker in the school. Now Regan's gone from popular princess to total pariah. The only person who speaks to her is former best-friend's hot-but-socially-miscreant brother, Nolan Letner. And the consequences of Regan's fall from grace are only just beginning. Once the chain reaction starts, no one will remain untouched...

Lola Carlyle's 12-Step Romance
by Danielle Younge-Ullman

While the idea of a summer in rehab is a terrible idea (especially when her biggest addiction is organic chocolate), Lola Carlyle finds herself tempted by the promise of spa-like accommodations and her major hottie crush. Unfortunately, Sunrise Rehabilitation Center isn't quite what she expected. Her best friend has gone AWOL, the facility is definitely more jail than spa, and boys are completely off-limits...except for Lola's infuriating(and irritatingly hot) mentor, Adam. Worse still, she might have found the one messy, invasive place where life actually makes sense.

LOVE AND OTHER UNKNOWN VARIABLES

BY SHANNON LEE ALEXANDER

Charlie Hanson has a clear vision of his future. A senior at Brighton School of Mathematics and Science, he knows he'll graduate, go to MIT, and inevitably discover the solutions to the universe's greatest unanswerable problems. But for Charlotte Finch, the future has never seemed very kind. Charlie's future blurs the moment he meets Charlotte, but by the time he learns Charlotte is ill, her gravitational pull on him is too great to overcome. Soon he must choose between the familiar formulas he's always relied on or the girl he's falling for.